D1567553

WE'RE ALL DOOMED!

First published in Great Britain in 2009 by Prion
an imprint of the Carlton Publishing Group
20 Mortimer Street
London W1T 3JW

10 9 8 7 6 5 4 3 2 1

A catalogue record for this book is available from the British Library

ISBN 978-1-85375-707-5

Printed in Dubai

WE'RE ALL DOOMED!

A LIGHT-HEARTED GUIDE TO THE FORTHCOMING MULTI-APOCALYPSE

by Mike Haskins

Illustrations by Mike Mosedale

PRION

CONTENTS

INTRODUCTION 9

COMING YOUR WAY SOON!

Destruction of the Rainforest	10
Meteorite/ Asteroid Collision	12
Viral Pandemic	14
World Water Shortage	16
Rising Sea Levels	18
Super-volcano Eruption	20
Terrorism	22
Unsustainable Lifestyles	24

IT'S HAPPENING ALREADY

Economic Meltdown	26
Antibiotic Resistance	28
Climate Change	30
Colony Collapse Disorder	32
Ozone Depletion	34
Famine	36
Oil Shortage	38
Overpopulation	40
Pollution	42

"OK lady... If you wanna see another day, hand over that
stolen honey you got from the store earlier."

CONTENTS

DEFINITELY CAN'T BE RULED OUT

Loss of Breathable Atmosphere 44

Breakdown of the Gulf Stream 46

Bubonic Plague 48

Changes in Planetary Movement 50

Cosmic Radiation 52

Decline of Fertility 54

GM Crops Take Over The World 56

HIV 58

Human Extinction 60

Mega-tsunami 62

Polar Shift 64

Black Holes 66

IT'S GOING TO HAPPEN BUT NOT JUST YET

Big Crunch 68

Galaxy Collision 70

Ice Age 72

Explosion of the Sun 74

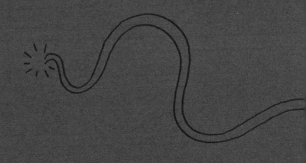

THINGS WE MIGHT EASILY BRING UPON OURSELVES

Artificially Created Diseases 76

Biological Weapons 78

Collapse of Ecosystems 80

Computers Take Over the World 82

De-evolution 84

Nuclear War 86

Grey Goo 88

E-Bomb 90

YEAH RIGHT!

Alien Invasion 92

Armageddon 94

Artificial Reality 96

Matter Suddenly Transforms... 98

Ragnarok 100

Scientific Experiments... 102

Mayan Calendar 104

The Rapture 106

FINALLY AND SLIGHTLY MORE OPTIMISTICALLY

We're Not Doomed... Are We? 110

PREPARE
TO MEET
THY DOOM

mosedale

INTRODUCTION

Since the dawn of time man has been obsessed with his own end. That's men for you. At least it helped take their minds off worrying about the world coming to an end. In previous centuries our forebears were terrified that the world would be destroyed at any moment.

Today we know that it was ignorance and superstition that led them to fear that the sky would fall on their heads or that the millennium bug would crash their computers.Yes, our primitive forebears were absolute amateurs compared to us today.

Today we enjoy a much greater choice of ways in which the world could end. Not only that, but there's an excellent chance that some of them will actually work this time. Some may come about as a result of scientific phenomena that we will be completely powerless to prevent. Obviously this has given us all a terrible feeling of helplessness. In order to overcome this, we have therefore developed a range of ways in which we can destroy the world

ourselves either by accident or on purpose as the mood takes us. And if we don't get round to any of those, we are of course all currently helping to destroy the environment a little bit at a time. Each and every day each of us is working to make our world completely uninhabitable. Who said that all mankind could never collaborate on such a major project?

Of course we know it's not sensible to keep polluting and destroying our entire planet the way we are but none of the alternatives seem terribly attractive or convenient so what else can we do? And if all else fails to destroy us we still have a whole host of ignorant, superstitious beliefs also hoping for a slice of end-of-the-world action.

So today thanks to advances in science none of us need ever again lie in a cold sweat at night worrying about whether or not we really are doomed. Because we are. Definitely. Thanks for that, science. That's really put our minds at rest.

DESTRUCTION OF THE RAINFOREST

Cutting down the Amazon rainforest is already causing one consequence even more disastrous than global warming. Every single day, rainforest destruction releases a vast cloud of environmental statistics into the atmosphere. Gradually these horrifying facts and figures will build up until an immense statistical tidal wave is sent crashing across the world like a great factoid tsunami.

There is a type of extreme pubic hair wrenching for ladies called a Brazilian. The reason it is called a Brazilian is because this is what the Amazon rainforest will look like in a few years time: a long, very thin strip of tatty vegetation with an unattractively sore looking area on either side.

By the middle of the century the Amazon rainforest will be about half the size it originally was. Fifty years after that it will consist of a small pot plant in a garden centre outside Rio de Janeiro. Over the past 50 years we have managed to destroy an area of Amazon rainforest the size of France and Germany. This has led many to ask if it wouldn't have been better to just destroy France and Germany.

Nearly half the world's plant, animal and insect species will be destroyed with the loss of the rainforest. We are currently losing 137 species every single day. And that's just plain careless.

The rainforest is of course being cut down to create farming land. Unfortunately once you get rid of the trees it turns out that the soil underneath is extremely poor. This means you can only grow things on it for about ten minutes. That's why they keep cutting down more and more rainforest. It's like having a strip of one-use, disposable farms that you simply throw away when you've finished with them.

Cutting down the rainforest creates about 18% of global greenhouse gas emissions. This is the same as the entire emissions from the USA, the worst polluter in the world. This means that we have managed to convert the oxygen producing, life sustaining rainforest into the joint worst polluter in the world! And we think we're the most intelligent creatures on the planet!

TELLTALE SIGNS IT'S HAPPENING
- The climate will become extraordinarily uncomfortable
- Oxygen may have to be rationed
- Even worse, products such as coffee and chocolate will be in short supply

WHERE NOT TO STAND
- Under any segment of rainforest scheduled for the chop
- Anywhere else on the planet

HOW TO AVOID THE PROBLEM

• Create your own personal biosphere by wearing a diver's helmet with a mini rainforest growing inside it

• Tell everyone you meet, "You know that rainforest thing. Do you think it would be a good idea if we kept that?"

LOOK ON THE BRIGHT SIDE

• Brazil will have enough clear space to build the biggest patio area the world has ever seen

HOW TO AVOID THE PROBLEM
• Get yourself a really really strong umbrella or hat
• Practise your football heading skills and build up until you reach the point where you can deflect large, semi-molten boulders

LOOK ON THE BRIGHT SIDE
• Definitely no more dinosaurs after this one

METEORITE AND/OR ASTEROID COLLISION

An asteroid about seven miles (10 km) across hit us 65 million years ago. If you want to know how much damage it did, ask a dinosaur next time you see one.

If an object even about a mile (1.6 km) across flies from out of space and smacks into the Earth, it's seriously bad news particularly if you try to catch it and you're not wearing gloves. Fortunately we only get hit by objects this size once every million years. Slightly less fortunately the next one is due on October 26, 2028.

Scientists now however assure us that this asteroid (35396) 1997 XF11 will safely miss us by 579,000 miles (933,000 km). Mind you scientists also once believed kipper ties were the height of fashion, so what do they know? Nevertheless 1997 XF11 is just the size of asteroid that could do serious damage to us. And things do keep bumping into us.

A particularly clumsy asteroid travelling at a speed of seven miles per second (10 km/sec) is believed to have ploughed into the earth's atmosphere on June 30, 1908. The resulting explosion was equivalent to 10 to 15 million tonnes of TNT and completely flattened an area 1.3 times the size of Greater London. Luckily this happened in Siberia where the main casualties were 80 million trees and many suggested the collision actually helped improve the area.

This event in Tunguska, Siberia is believed to have been caused by an asteroid less than 85 yards (75 m) across. So in other words it was a fun-sized asteroid.

We expect to be hit by one of these every 100 years which is a less than comforting thought when we've just passed the 100th anniversary of the last one.

Even objects a mere five to ten yards in size cause explosions equivalent to the atomic bomb dropped on Hiroshima when they hit the atmosphere. They do this about once per year and yet hardly anyone seems to notice.

So if your house looks like it's been hit by an atomic bomb, that could be the reason why.

TELLTALE SIGNS IT'S HAPPENING
- Everyone will be pointing at the sky and screaming
- It will be quite difficult to miss

WHERE NOT TO STAND
- Under any rapidly growing round shadows

13

VIRAL PANDEMIC

Nature is the world's ultimate bio-terrorist. So the only way to recognize a deadly pandemic is to look at a sample under the microscope and see if the microbes all have little beards and/or are wearing tiny balaclavas...

Viral pandemics sweep round the world every century killing millions. One strain of flu emerged in 1918 and killed more people than the First World War. It was a bit like a telesales call. Not only did no-one want it but it happened at a really inconvenient moment. By 1920 between 20 and 40 million people had suffered rapid and horrible deaths. One physician recalled that sufferers "died struggling to clear their airways of a blood-tinged froth that sometimes gushed from their nose and mouth." And that's unlikely to make it into any list of the top five most popular ways to die.

Another global viral pandemic will inevitably happen at some point. Governments around the world say they have drawn up detailed plans of actions of how to deal with such a crisis. This would be reassuring if it weren't for the fact that we've seen some of their previous attempts to deal with crises.

In recent years bird flu has killed millions of birds. It has also killed a few hundred people. While humans are completely terrified by bird flu, you never hear any birds openly voicing concern about the matter. Nevertheless, humans still have the audacity to use the expression "chicken" to denote a cowardly person.

The current strain of bird flu may mutate so it can be transmitted from human to human rather than from sneezing bird to human. If it does so bird flu could kill every single one of us. Things could then be made even worse particularly if the thought of dying of bird flu causes us all to get "The Birdy Song" tune stuck in our heads just as we are breathing our last.

But of course bird flu will not really kill us all. Pandemics always carefully avoid finishing off every one of their potential victims.

After all, they've got to leave a few of us so they can make a comeback tour a couple of years later.

TELLTALE SIGNS IT'S HAPPENING

- Your doctor will be wearing a biological protection suit when you go for a check-up
- Birds will appear every time you are near but unfortunately they will be falling out of the sky on you

WHERE NOT TO STAND

- Next to a sneezing chicken

HOW TO AVOID THE PROBLEM
- Avoid close contact with birds
- Avoid sticking your head inside poultry for supposed comic effect
- Also avoid people who have been in long term intimate relationships with birds (eg Keith Harris and Orville)

LOOK ON THE BRIGHT SIDE
- Chicken dippers will be off the menu

HOW TO AVOID THE PROBLEM
• Set up your own mini filtration and bottling plant in your toilet

LOOK ON THE BRIGHT SIDE
• Who knows, you might develop a taste for urine

16

WORLD WATER SHORTAGE

Somehow we've managed to reach a situation where we face both a crisis from not having enough water and a crisis from flooding. There's nothing more frustrating than having to put up with a hosepipe ban when your living room is under six feet (1.8 m) of water.

Water covers over 70% of the earth's surface. It has been estimated there are 326 million trillion gallons of water on earth. It is therefore testament to man's extraordinary ingenuity that a major water shortage is looming!

But, as those in the Third World might say, "What do you mean 'looming'?"

Already, a third of the world's population live in what are termed "water stressed" areas. By 2050 this will have risen to two thirds. That's a lot of stressed water. And if the water is getting stressed, people will surely be feeling a bit hot under the collar as well.

Lack of water in some areas of the world is believed to significantly contribute to increasing terrorism and war. So if only we all had the chance to have a soak in a lovely hot bath every night, the world would be a more peaceful place and would smell of bubble bath. Well, it might be more peaceful as long as we remember to leave the bathroom as we would like to find it.

The lack of water doesn't just mean we'll feel a bit thirsty and face constant horrible wars without being able to have a shower afterwards. A lack of water will also mean a devastating lack of food. In the west 70% of the water we get through isn't used for drinking but in food production.

And for any of those who say they never drink water because fish make love in it, water is vital to us. A human being will collapse after only three days without it. This is because we are literally made of water. Adult females are around 55% water while adult males are 60% water.

So don't forget, if you ever get really thirsty you're best off squeezing an adult male in your juicer.

TELLTALE SIGNS IT'S HAPPENING

- There will be no water anywhere –fairly difficult to miss
- People will either be dying or commenting that they're a bit thirsty
- If you happen break out in a sweat strangers will start licking you

WHERE NOT TO STAND

- In the middle of the hysterical mob gathered in the bottled water aisle of the supermarket

17

RISING SEA LEVELS

If you've always fancied living near the sea but live miles inland, it's good news! Soon the sea will be coming to you!

How can the sea level be rising? Has someone left the taps running somewhere? Are we not drinking enough to use all the water up? Are we drinking too much so we're filling the sea by going to the toilet too often?

The obvious reason why sea levels are rising is because of our old friend, global warming.

Climate change is causing the world's ice caps and glaciers to melt at a rate which has been officially expressed as, "quicker than we were expecting" and, "wellies on, everyone!"

Another slightly more unexpected problem is that the global rise in temperatures is causing the water that is already in the oceans to warm up. And as water warms up, it expands. So not only

are we all going to drown, we're going to drown in water that seems unnaturally big to us. At least it should be nice and warm.

It is believed that sea levels could rise by about 4' 11" (1.5 m) over the next century. Many people (particularly those who are over 5" tall) remain apparently unconcerned and seem to think that the loss of low lying areas such as Holland and their downstairs rooms may be a price worth paying.

They assume that measures can be taken to avoid the problems of sea level rise. If all else fails we can all move to live on the tops of mountains or, as they will soon be re-named, islands. So it's typical isn't it? It took us millions of years to evolve and get ourselves out of the sea. Now we've wrecked the place so badly the sea's coming to take us back.

TELLTALE SIGNS IT'S HAPPENING

- Damp lapping sensation around your ankles everywhere you go
- Or, even worse, a damp lapping sensation round your neck
- All TV news reports will feature a reporter in wellies standing in some water even when they're just doing the sports results

WHERE NOT TO STAND

- Anywhere you notice a damp lapping sensation round your forehead

HOW TO AVOID THE PROBLEM
- Develop gills
- Start sporting extremely high platform shoes

LOOK ON THE BRIGHT SIDE
- You can re-name your house "Sea View"

HOW TO AVOID THE PROBLEM
● Apply several trillion tons of acne treatment to Yellowstone park

LOOK ON THE BRIGHT SIDE
● It's a bit of a spring-clean for the planet
● You won't be short of pumice stone – in fact you could find you are made of pumice stone

SUPER-VOLCANO ERUPTION

A super-volcano is an extraordinarily huge underground volcano, which under normal circumstances you would never notice was there. So it's a kind of stealth volcano.

Unfortunately there are a number of these underground oceans of boiling magma around the place and they do go off every now and then with cataclysmic results of global proportions.

Most recently a super-volcano in the vicinity of New Zealand erupted about 26,500 years ago. Even today New Zealand is still struggling to regain the pre-eminence in world affairs it enjoyed before this event.

An eruption in Indonesia 75,000 years ago is believed to have wiped out 60% of the human population of the planet. Don't worry – none of those people were closely related to you. In fact they're not related to anyone. Well, not anyone alive today.

Perhaps most worrying of all is the Yellowstone Cadera beneath Yellowstone Park in the USA. Obviously if this one blows it will be an enormous tragedy for the world not least because its first victims will inevitably be famous Yellowstone residents Yogi Bear, Boo Boo and Ranger Smith.

The Yellowstone super-volcano is 43 miles (70 km) by 18 miles (30 km). So if it erupts while you're standing in the middle of it, it will be quite difficult to run away from. Particularly as your legs will have just melted beneath you.

The Yellowstone explosion will destroy the USA before plunging the world into a new Ice Age. Isn't that always the way? You get rid of one problem only to immediately get landed with another.

An expert on the subject of the Yellowstone super-volcano has predicted it will explode in 2074. Or in other words about 30 years after the expert expects to die peacefully at home in his sleep... and about five minutes before the rest of us all die – not quite so peacefully.

TELLTALE SIGNS IT'S HAPPENING
- Sense of molten rock gently lapping about your ankles
- The USA (or some other equally large area) will suddenly cease to exist
- The sun obliterated by a black cloud even though your neighbours aren't having a barbecue

WHERE NOT TO STAND
- In the middle of any major eruptions if you can possibly help it

TERRORISM

Terrorists enjoy nothing better than coming up with increasingly unpleasant ways of killing increasingly large numbers of people. Devastating a large portion of the planet would be an ultimate act of terrorism and there must therefore be some keen terrorists out there with "destroy the Earth!" on their "to do" lists.

On September 20, 2001 President George W. Bush said he was declaring a "war on terror". This was somewhat ironic because wars tend to provoke quite a bit of terror themselves and rarely engender widespread feelings of calmness, relaxation and serenity.

Despite the war on terror and the fact that if you are terrified this theoretically means the entire US Army is at war with you, no-one in the world really knows what a terrorist is.

Yes, there is no internationally accepted definition of terrorism. The concept originally dates from the Reign of Terror during the French Revolution. This is why to this day you are not allowed to board an aeroplane carrying a large guillotine as part of your hand luggage.

For years terrorists contented themselves with assassinating the occasional archduke or hijacking the odd plane. Then in the 1970s they seemed to become increasingly violent, increasingly unpleasant, increasingly unapologetic and increasingly bearded. At some point somebody must have made the mistake of saying, "If these terrorists are so keen on blowing everything up, why don't they just blow themselves up!" They then started adopting this as a regular tactic.

With the September 11 attacks it became clear that terrorists today must be under the misapprehension that the most appalling atrocities imaginable are, in fact, really good ideas.

Negotiation with latter-day fundamentalist terrorists is also difficult. They seem to want nothing less than for every single person in the world who doesn't agree with everything they say to kill themselves. And that's something that even the best peace negotiators would baulk at signing up to.

In a sense though, terrorists' main objective in committing atrocities seems to be to get themselves as much TV airtime as possible. As such, terrorists are working along similar lines to marketing executives albeit with marginally less respect for human life and less use of jingles (unless of course you count the warbly music they play in on their dodgy internet videos).

TELLTALE SIGNS IT'S HAPPENING
• Tabloid newspapers start using the term "Bastards!" in their front page headlines

WHERE NOT TO STAND
• Just about anywhere
• Next to any shifty-looking men who seem to be making a loud ticking noise

22

HOW TO AVOID THE PROBLEM
- You may be safest if you hang around near older terrorists because usually they're the ones who get to stay behind and just make videos
- If they're this desperate for publicity just give them their own prime time Saturday night TV show called something like *Strictly Bin Laden* or *The Al Qaeda Factor*

LOOK ON THE BRIGHT SIDE
- Apparently some of them get rewarded with virgins in heaven

"Would you like a hand unwrapping your shopping ?"

HOW TO AVOID THE PROBLEM
- You could try living sustainably and then when you've finished doing that you could recycle yourself
- Get hold of a couple of fresh new planets to plunder (it will be quite difficult to find anywhere to put them though)

LOOK ON THE BRIGHT SIDE
- It only took us a few years to use up all of the planet's resources but never mind, it was fun while it lasted

UNSUSTAINABLE LIFESTYLES

Gandhi once said the world contains enough for every man's need but not for every man's greed. Although now Gandhi himself is no longer with us there is at least one more loin cloth to go round.

The natural cycle of things involves constant regeneration. Things live, they die and they get eaten by other things although not always necessarily in that order. At some point humankind made the understandable decision to opt out of the being-eaten-by-other-things part of the scheme. That part of the circle of life has never really been popular with anyone which is why it isn't even mentioned in the Disney song of the same name.

Humans are consumers of the resources of planet Earth. There are however more and more humans to consume these resources every year. The supply of resources was apparently so great that we thought we better keep producing more and more of ourselves to help get through it all.

Our insatiable demand for food, water, fuel and timber means we are eating, drinking and burning our way through all of the Earth's resources. So very soon it will be necessary to throw the planet away and start on another new one. Admittedly there doesn't seem to be another one readily available but we can always cross that bridge when we come to it.

The problem is that we keep converting the available resources of the planet into human beings. This means eventually we will have nothing left unless we start eating each other. This is usually frowned upon in polite society although it does offer a great opportunity for a new range of cookery books and specialist celebrity chefs.

Still, don't worry about the fact that we've completely exhausted the planet's energy, mineral and food reserves leaving nothing for future generations to survive on. Instead just look on it as a little challenge we've set for our kids!

TELLTALE SIGNS IT'S HAPPENING
• If anything breaks down or runs out you won't be able to replace it
• We will be given the bill for all the stuff we've kept taking from nature

WHERE NOT TO STAND
• On planet Earth

25

ECONOMIC MELTDOWN

John Paul Getty once said, "If you owe the bank $100 that's your problem. If you owe the bank $100 million, that's the bank's problem." The world's banks have now managed to successfully bypass both of these problems by achieving a situation where they all owe each other billions. This brilliantly makes it a problem for all of us — even if we don't have a bank account!

A credit crisis has engulfed the world. It threatens to bring down banks, financial institutions and even governments. This means entire populations may soon have their countries re-possessed. Essentially what has happened is that the world's banks have made their money by lending to each other. Unfortunately one day one of them made the fatal error of saying, "Actually do you know what? I don't really have any money!" At which point all the other banks said, "Neither have we. We were all working on the assumption that you had all the money."

As the rest of us had suspected for some time, the world's major financial institutions didn't actually have any real money. News reports about the crisis started referring to the rest of us as "the real economy" which clearly implied that the banks and financial institutions were "the completely fictitious, pretend economy."

Presumably if any of these financiers had ever had any real money they had spent it all on computer screens, red braces, hard drugs and the throat lozenges they needed after spending all day shouting, "Sell!" These people also of course require vast quantities of deodorant because the economic system is entirely based on confidence. In other words the world's entire financial systems have been entrusted to the greediest, least moral individuals on Earth who have turned it all into a big competition to see who will sweat the least under pressure. On the plus side, most of us don't seem in the least bit bothered about the collapse of the entire global financial system. This is because none of us understand much about finance and believe that our ignorance will protect us from the economic turmoil in the same way that closing your eyes makes you invisible.

It might therefore be an idea for government to start physically blowing up any banks that fail in the hope this would help convey the scale of the problem to us. Instead, they've hit on the idea of just handing us the bill for the whole sorry mess.

TELLTALE SIGNS IT'S HAPPENING

• The heads of all major financial organisations will award themselves even bigger bonuses than usual
• You will receive the bill for the entire thing on your next credit card statement

WHERE NOT TO STAND

• Anywhere in the financial sector particularly beneath any high windows

HOW TO AVOID THE PROBLEM
- Start your own currency based on the Bambara groundnut

LOOK ON THE BRIGHT SIDE
- You don't have to worry about getting a pay rise ever again
- You could pick up your very own multi-national bank at a bargain price at a car boot sale

27

HOW TO AVOID THE PROBLEM
• Try and be a bit more selective about any diseases you catch

LOOK ON THE BRIGHT SIDE
• No more nasty tasting medicine

RESISTANCE TO ANTIBIOTIC MEDICINES

Terrible deadly infections are becoming increasingly resistant to treatment antibiotics. Soon the worst effect that antibiotic medicine will be able to have on E. Coli will be when it complains about the horrible taste...

Modern antibiotics began with Sir Alexander Fleming's discovery of penicillin in 1928. Fleming's discovery was apparently due to his failure to clean up the culture dishes in his laboratory properly when he was studying staphylococci. He noticed an area of mould that had stopped the bacteria growing on the dish and he really sat up and took notice when he saw it walk across his laboratory and make itself a sandwich. Fleming is therefore one of the very few people to have been awarded the Nobel Prize because they couldn't bothered doing the dishes. Ironically when he held a dinner party to celebrate the discovery of penicillin all his guests died from food poisoning over the next few days.

There are now many types of different antibiotics and they have been used to save millions of lives. Or to put it another way, if antibiotics were to stop working for any reason millions of us would die.

And indeed the widespread use of antibiotics has led to some bacterial infections developing a resistance to them. Microorganisms are capable of evolving at an extraordinary rate and because we've been stuffing ourselves and our livestock with antibiotics for the past 80 years, they have inevitably mutated by natural selection into resistant forms. Creationists who don't believe in evolution will however obviously be completely immune to this problem.

The resulting so called super-bugs are potentially lethal. Not only are they capable of resisting treatment with antibiotics but they have afterwards been observed attempting to shove the empty pill bottle up the backside of the doctor who prescribed them.

So could all of humanity be wiped out by antibiotic resistant super-bugs? It is possible but it would depend on all of us being confined to the same hospital ward at some point.

TELLTALE SIGNS IT'S HAPPENING

- People will start dying of things that people don't usually die of e.g. tonsillitis, toothache, sprained ankle etc
- Doctors will have to go back to applying leeches

WHERE NOT TO STAND

- Near anyone infectious
- Near any super-bugs

CLIMATE CHANGE

Over recent decades carbon dioxide from, for example, transportation has been released into the atmosphere in massive amounts. This has caused a rapid and potentially catastrophic rise in global temperatures. Luckily the automotive industry has been quick to develop a solution to the problem: in-car air conditioning.

At first everyone thought that climate change was a great idea. Nobody was happy with the climate they had. People hated the climate, they moaned about the climate and spent all their time saving up their money so they could go on holiday to anywhere that had a better climate. When TV weather forecasters said there was a chance of rain, they had to do so while looking ashen-faced as though they were about to be taken out and publicly flogged. Which of course they often were.

By incredible good fortune, the greenhouse gas emissions produced by all the cars, boats and planes carrying people to the places that had better climates had a direct effect on the overall climate. It began to get warmer! This should have made everyone happy but of course it didn't. Instead everyone is now getting hot under the collar. In fact scientists predict they could be as much as 3.5° Celsius (118.3° F) hotter under the collar by the end of the century.

People are in a panic about the mess we've made of the world's weather systems. If we wanted to adjust the world's temperature why didn't we just install a simple thermostat dial somewhere near the equator? Instead the vast quantities of gases such as carbon dioxide and methane we have pumped into the atmosphere since the industrial revolution have caused the greenhouse effect. This means that Mother Earth is, like many middle aged women, now beginning to get warmer and less stable.

There are some who deny the existence of the greenhouse effect and say that there is no link between the massive increase in global temperatures and the massive increase in gases we are producing. By a massive coincidence these people usually work for the oil or gas industries. Clearly the only solution is for them to be locked inside a greenhouse with a running petrol engine. Then eventually they might begin to grasp the concept.

TELLTALE SIGNS IT'S HAPPENING
- The climate will change
- The weather will seem to have had a nervous breakdown

WHERE NOT TO STAND
- Too near any weather forecasters about to be lynched because "it's all their fault"
- Near any environmentalists anxious to let you know that they "told you so"

"Shut the door...it's another ten minutes before your turn."

HOW TO AVOID THE PROBLEM
• Move somewhere that doesn't really have a climate

LOOK ON THE BRIGHT SIDE
• The weather will be a constant surprise

HOW TO AVOID THE PROBLEM
• Train other more readily available creatures (e.g. otters, cats, boy scouts) to do the job of pollinating the millions of plants in your neighbourhood (n.b. this may require significant amounts of time and patience)
• Try living off non-pollinated produce (eg potatoes, instant noodles etc)

LOOK ON THE BRIGHT SIDE
• At least you're probably not going to get stung... except by wasps

COLONY COLLAPSE DISORDER

Politicians obviously aren't that important. Celebrities we can live without. The people who run the local shop are quite useful but somewhat unexpectedly our survival depends on small yellow and black stingy insects. And unfortunately they now all seem to be buzzing off. They're dying in vast numbers!

Who'd have thought it? We're all dependent on little buzzy bees for our continued survival. Why? Because bee pollinate plants. Yes, due to a slight oversight in government planning the process of food production has been entrusted to creatures with brains the size of pinheads. And these people at the Department for Agriculture have in turn passed responsibility on to bees.

Across the USA and Europe beekeepers keep turning up to their hives only to find all their bees have mysteriously disappeared. And no-one is entirely sure why. It could be something to do with the way we've been treating bees all these years. If they really are the most important creatures on the planet, was it sensible for us to keep dressing up in scary suits and masks whenever we went near them before blasting them with smoke and running off with all their honey? A honey bee will only produce one twelfth of a teaspoon of honey over its lifetime. So it's little comfort for them to look down from bee heaven and see one of us spreading their life's work over a very small piece of toast. No wonder then if the little fellas are a tiny bit peeved with us.

Many theories have been put forward for the disappearance of bees among them the growing use of mobile phones. Either the bees are being thrown off track and getting lost because of the preponderance of mobile phone signals in the atmosphere, or alternatively they've learnt to use mobile phones themselves.

Now every time they see a masked smoking giant coming to towards their hive intent on a smash and grab on their and 50,000 of their closest friends and family's life work, they phone each other up and say, "Quick! The bastards are coming again! Everyone scarper!"

TELLTALE SIGNS IT'S HAPPENING
- You'll be knee deep in dead bees
- A jar of honey will cost as much as your house

WHERE NOT TO STAND
- On top of the world's last living bee

33

OZONE DEPLETION

We have been told for decades that a massive hole in the Earth's ozone layer opens up over Antarctica every year. So far though very few people have fallen out of it...

Ozone is a type of oxygen molecule. These are irritating, corrosive pollutants that can cause us serious lung damage. The ozone molecules obviously all felt slightly guilty about this and decided to band together in the cause of good. And so they formed the ozone layer.

Ozone forms a protective layer around the Earth that keeps out ultraviolet rays coming from the sun. If these rays reach us they can blind us which would at least prevent us from seeing that they had also covered us with skin cancer.

The ozone layer was discovered in 1913. In 1930, just 17 years after discovering this wonderfully helpful, protective and naturally occurring part of the stratosphere, mankind decided to invent chlorofluorocarbons. These turned out to be slightly less helpful. Chlorofluorocarbon is fantastic news but only if you get it as a hand in Scrabble. This good news is slightly outweighed by the fact that it destroys the planet's life preserving ozone layer. Discovery of this fact made people very tense

which then caused them to use even more aerosol deodorant which obviously didn't help matters.

By the 1970s the world had discovered that it had a bit less of an ozone layer and a bit more of a CFC layer. Having so much CFC in the atmosphere was dangerous because if a madman ever installed a huge push-down plastic cap on top of the Earth it would spray the entire atmosphere into space like a huge planet-sized aerosol. People began to heed warnings over the ozone. They gave up using CFCs so much and stopped sunbathing immediately beneath the ozone hole in Antarctica.

A few years ago the ozone layer was going to cause the end of the world by turning us all into a pile of well roasted malignant melanomas. Today it's still going to end the world but because it's lulled us into a false sense of security that we can sort out the other threats to the planet just like we did with the ozone problem.

How was it we did it again? Of course! It was by putting that giant planet-sized toupee on the atmosphere wasn't it? Not only did that help save the ozone layer, it had the additional benefit of making the Earth look a few billion years younger than it really is.

TELLTALE SIGNS IT'S HAPPENING

- There will be a vast hole in the ozone layer
- The word "melanoma" will crop up regularly in conversation

WHERE NOT TO STAND

- Directly under the vast hole in the ozone layer
- Anywhere on planet Earth during daylight hours

HOW TO AVOID THE PROBLEM
- Live underground
- Apply factor 50 sun lotion all over your radiation suit

LOOK ON THE BRIGHT SIDE
- People won't be so keen to show off their suntans to you

"Look! There's some over there."

HOW TO AVOID THE PROBLEM
• You could publish a book entitled *101 Recipes For Cannibals*

LOOK ON THE BRIGHT SIDE
• You'll have the same build as a supermodel

FAMINE

The prospect of famine looms over all of us. Of course a lot of people in the west currently eat very poor, high fat diets so a shortage of food might do them quite a bit of good. So ironically by the time they're dropping dead of starvation, they could be in a healthier state than they are at the moment.

Terrible famine will surely sweep across the world in the coming century. It will be caused by a combination of the effects of climate change, drought, pestilence, exhaustion of the soil, lack of pesticides and fertilizers after our oil supplies run out, economic collapse and overpopulation. In fact taking all that into account it's a wonder there's any food around now. The unfortunate truth of course is that for many people around the world there already isn't. And as a range of catastrophic environmental and overpopulation factors kick in over the next few years the starving people sector of the population is one that is certainly going to see continued growth. So if you like eating food even occasionally, you better start stuffing yourself now.

Obviously a lot of people have instinctively already begun doing this in the expectation that not only will their morbid obesity help them survive the forthcoming agricultural crisis, they could also win Slimmer of the Year in the process. There will however be quite a lot of competition for this title in a world where none of us have any food.

Similarly anyone who's recently lost a fantastic amount of weight on an amazing new diet will soon be bitterly regretting their squandered fat reserves and will start investigating the possibility of suing their diet programme adviser.

People remain strangely unconcerned that 12.5% of the world's population already don't have enough to eat. If this percentage doubles just three times it will mean we are all starving. Obviously though we will never reach this point. There will always be at least one person left with enough money to sit in comfort while watching the rest of us starve. Who knows, if we're lucky he might even record a charity single for us.

TELLTALE SIGNS IT'S HAPPENING
- Starvation, panic and complete social breakdown
- Supermarkets will have nothing on the shelves
- Michael Moore will start to look slightly thinner

WHERE NOT TO STAND
- Next to any obese people just before they keel over

OIL SHORTAGE

The formation of fossil fuels like oil takes millions of years. So when current supplies run out there's going to be one hell of a wait at the petrol station for the next lot to be ready

Europe and the USA do not produce enough oil for their own needs. China has recently become the second largest user of oil in the world. Demand is growing by 15% a year. This would be great news for the oil industry apart from one slight snag: it's a finite resource and no-one knows exactly how much is left. This is odd because we get through around 31.5 billion gallons (143 billion litres) of oil a year. What's more our jobs, health, food, energy, national security and economies are all completely dependent on the stuff. And yet we haven't made any proper plans for what we'll do when supplies run out and for all we know that could be a week next Tuesday! What crazy, happy-go-lucky, care-free folks we must be!

The oil industry has nevertheless tried to reassure us by saying reserves exist for the next 40 years. This is not actually that reassuring because they told us exactly the same thing 30 years ago. Maybe the oil industry isn't being very specific. When they say they have enough oil for 40 years, perhaps what they mean is there's enough for an old age pensioner with a moped that she only uses at weekends. And it's not just luxuries we can do without like cars, hospitals and national defence systems that run on oil. All of us eat oil every day!

Every single step in the food production process involves petrochemicals or other fossil fuels. Pesticides are made from oil, fertilizers are made from natural gas and, as yet, very few farmers use pedal powered tractors. Food storage systems are also powered by fossil fuels and our food comes wrapped in plastics made from oil.

Without oil we'll have nothing to eat. And even if we did, it will have gone off by the time it gets to us. And it won't get to us because there won't be any transport to deliver it to the shops. Or, for that matter, for us to go to the shops and buy it.

We are therefore currently involved in a critical race against time. Will our society collapse because the world's oil reserves run out? Or will there be enough for us to carry on burning it until we've completely destroyed the atmosphere?

TELLTALE SIGNS IT'S HAPPENING

- Total collapse of civilization
- Rioting in the streets
- Long queue at the petrol station

WHERE NOT TO STAND

- At the front of the queue for the last litre of petrol

38

HOW TO AVOID THE PROBLEM
- Carve a large hole in the bottom of your car and keep driving Fred Flintstone-style
- Re-discover the ancient art of moving around by continually putting one foot in front of the other

LOOK ON THE BRIGHT SIDE
- The air will be nice and clean

HOW TO AVOID THE PROBLEM
• Try reducing the population by making your-self very unattractive to the opposite sex (less of a challenge to some of us than others)

LOOK ON THE BRIGHT SIDE
• You'll never be lonely

OVERPOPULATION

If we are extraordinarily lucky and no other disasters hit us that still leaves the planet's single biggest problem. And if you want to know what that is, try looking in the mirror.

It took the human population of the Earth hundreds of thousands of years to build up to one billion strong. It finally achieved this figure in 1804. Having now got the hang of the process, the human race managed to add another billion in a mere 123 years hitting two billion in 1927. Productivity continued to increase and just twenty years later in 1947 we reached the four billion mark. Can you spot the problem yet? Yes, the human race is currently performing the planetary equivalent of one of those world record attempts to see how many people you can fit inside a Mini.

There are 200,000 new members of the human race added every single day. That's why General Michael Hayden, director of the CIA, has said that overpopulation rather than terrorism or global warming is the biggest threat facing the world. We are quite literally our own worst enemy. One study has suggested that the USA needs to reduce its population by a third to achieve a sustainable level. The same (presumably American) study says the rest of the world also needs to reduce its population – but by two thirds! Presumably this is because the one third of Americans that need to go weigh the same amount as the two thirds of everyone else.

So ironically the conclusion seems to be that in order for the planet to survive we need to go. Clearly the only hope is if we start actively encouraging some of the other disaster scenarios in this book! There are said to be so many of us alive now that we need the resources of three planets to sustain us rather than one. Actually better make that four planets because we've already buggered the one we've got haven't we?

TELLTALE SIGNS IT'S HAPPENING
- It will be crowded absolutely everywhere, even in church
- The only thing not in short supply will be people

WHERE NOT TO STAND
- Underneath everybody else

POLLUTION

There are three main types of pollution: air pollution, water pollution and land pollution. In other words we've stuffed things up for the birds, the fishes and, most brilliantly of all, for ourselves.

As well as air, water and land pollution we've now also created noise pollution, light pollution and thermal pollution. Obviously just polluting the air we breathe, the water we drink and the land we stand on wasn't good enough and we had to start coming up with brand new forms of pollution. Yes, our houses may all be lovely, clean and tidy but that's because we've spent the past few hundred years filling the rest of the world with all the rubbish we keep pumping out in such vast quantities.

We've tried burning our waste, which adds to global warming. We've tried dumping it in the sea but this tends to mean we get to eat it all a few months later when it comes back in a tasty fish and crispy crumb coating. And we've tried the industrial scale equivalent of brushing our rubbish under the carpet by burying it in landfill sites. The world is now so stuffed full of our disgusting rubbish it could burst over us at any moment like the most enormous rancid spot in history.

We have transformed the entire world into a vast waste dump. This means that we may ultimately all receive our comeuppance when we get pecked to death by all the seagulls flocking around it. All the rubbish we've produced during our lives is still out there in the world somewhere. Clearly some kind of system should be established to try and return all the junk in the world to its original owners. Ebay for example has done an exemplary job redistributing old crap and even managing to get its recipients to pay for the privilege.

TELLTALE SIGNS IT'S HAPPENING

- There will be nowhere left to throw any of our rubbish away
- When you open your windows piles of rubbish will fall into your house

WHERE NOT TO STAND

- Anywhere in the atmosphere

"Landfill Ho!"

HOW TO AVOID THE PROBLEM
• Stop producing any pollution
• Recycle everything, walk or cycle everywhere you go and don't break wind

LOOK ON THE BRIGHT SIDE
• It will be pointless trying to tidy up any more

HOW TO AVOID THE PROBLEM
- Practice holding your breath
- Get your local gas man to convert your respiratory system to accept CO2 instead

LOOK ON THE BRIGHT SIDE
- No more nasty niffs... well, no more niffs whatsoever

SUDDEN LOSS OF THE BREATHABLE ATMOSPHERE

Not much debate with this one is there? If the breathable atmosphere goes then the future of humanity will last no more than a few minutes and it will be those who are best at holding their breath who survive longest. Even more annoyingly this means that David Blaine will probably end up as the last surviving man on Earth.

If the world's breathable atmosphere suddenly disappears people will be shocked. Everyone will take a sharp intake of breath and this will quickly bring home the full extent of the problem. Some people will run around panicking but luckily they won't be able to do this for very long. Our leaders will go on television to make a formal announcement but will then decide to just stand in silence because saying anything would only make the situation worse. The rest of us will all have to stand around in silence perhaps giving the odd nod of the head or grimace to those near us until we all begin toppling over one by one.

The situation will be extremely difficult even for those who have had lots of practice at holding their breath from visiting recently vacated lavatories.

Worryingly the Earth is genuinely leaking oxygen into space like a punctured planet-sized beach ball. Luckily in space no-one can hear you scream, let alone the constant low pitched farting noise that our entire planet must be making as the air leaks out.

At present the amount of leaking oxygen is negligible but as the sun gets older and begins to heat up, the leaking oxygen problem could get worse. It is unclear however whether this will mean the Earth will fly madly around the solar system like a burst balloon for a few minutes before collapsing in a corner.

And in case you think this is all extremely unlikely, some experts believe it has already happened. Some scientists have suggested that the demise of the dinosaurs was not caused by asteroid impact but by a catastrophic loss of oxygen following a build up of carbon dioxide in the atmosphere. An enormous build up of carbon dioxide in the Earth's atmosphere! As if that could ever happen again!

TELLTALE SIGNS IT'S HAPPENING
- Breathe in. Any oxygen there? OK. It's not happened yet
- You will start to hear newsreaders using the phrase "the wholesale price of oxygen"
- Everyone around you will start turning purple

WHERE NOT TO STAND
- In the breathable atmosphere (because it won't be breathable)

45

BREAKDOWN OF THE GULF STREAM

The Gulf Stream, which brings the weather systems across the Atlantic that help make North West Europe inhabitable, is under threat of total breakdown. People are horrified when they hear this because if this is what the weather's like when the thing is working...

The Gulf Stream is an ocean current that acts as a conveyor belt bringing the warm air which makes North-Western Europe inhabitable. Although to be honest there are some areas in North-Western Europe that need a bit more than this. It would therefore be helpful if the Gulf Stream could try bringing some decent coffee shops and maybe a branch of Ikea as well.

As a result of global warming, some believe the Gulf Stream may be about to break down. This has been welcomed by many people who think the Atlantic conveyor has not been doing a particularly good job and that it is high time the whole thing was thrown open to competition.

Maybe another system will step in and start bringing some better weather.

The way the Gulf Stream is meant to operate is as follows: Arctic winds cool the water in the North Atlantic; this water becomes saltier, it sinks and heads south to the Gulf of Mexico; there it warms up again while pushing the warm waters of the gulf across the Atlantic towards Europe. Unfortunately the Atlantic now seems to have heard about salt not being very good for you and has decided to cut down on its intake. In fact the reason it's getting less salty is because it is being diluted by all the non-salty water coming from ice sheets that are melting because of global warming. Yes, it's all our fault yet again. It's another thing we've managed to break. If we've paid any kind of deposit on this planet, it doesn't look like we're going to get it back when we leave.

TELLTALE SIGNS IT'S HAPPENING
• Europe will become uninhabitable – OK even more uninhabitable

WHERE NOT TO STAND
• Europe – fairly obviously

"I'm afraid it looks like the Gulf is off this weekend."

HOW TO AVOID THE PROBLEM
• Try kick-starting the Gulf Stream again by pouring a large amount of salt into the Atlantic while paddling furiously with a piece of wood

LOOK ON THE BRIGHT SIDE
• Parking should be a lot easier in London

CHANGES IN PLANETARY MOVEMENT

If someone bumps into you on the pavement it can be uncomfortable. If they are in a car it's painful. If they are in a train it will be fatal. By the time you get to "if they are standing on another planet hurtling out of the sky towards you", things really aren't looking good.

The planets in our solar system are, as we know, all happily revolving around the sun. This is because the sun has a greater gravitational pull than any of the planets thanks to its much larger size. The sun is for example so big it could have a million Earths stuffed inside it although attempting to do this in practice would be both expensive and time consuming.

Jupiter is however also a very large object. Like young girls going out together, our planets realize it's a good idea to be accompanied by a friend who is larger than they are. Not only will this make them look slimmer by comparison but their bigger friend's huge gravitational pull will mean they are the ones who are more likely to get hit by stray passing asteroids. Jupiter's vast size is however threatening to destabilize the planet Mercury, the cosmic tiddler only 5% of the size of the Earth.

Scientists have identified four possible outcomes for what will happen if Jupiter dislodges Mercury from its orbit. Either Mercury will be thrown out of the solar system, Mercury will crash into the sun, Mercury will crash into Venus or Mercury will crash into Earth. Clumsy little sod isn't it?

Hang on! Did someone just say Mercury might crash into Earth? This would be good news for Mercury because people would stop remarking how small it was compared to other planets and instead concentrate on just how much bigger it was than anything else flying out of the sky towards us. If we get hit by an asteroid 1 mile (1.6 km) across it would be fairly disastrous to civilization. An asteroid about 6.2 miles (10 km) across wiped out the dinosaurs. Mercury is 3,032 miles (4,880 km) across.

The scientists who identified this problem have tried to reassure us by saying that there's only a 1% chance of Mercury crashing into us. Only a one in 100 chance that one of the other planets in the solar system will bash into us! That should help you sleep easy at night.

TELLTALE SIGNS IT'S HAPPENING
- Changes in gravity, atmospheric conditions and a noticeable increase in the number of planets hurtling out of the sky in your general direction

WHERE NOT TO STAND
- In the way of any hurtling planets
- On the surface of any hurtling planets

HOW TO AVOID THE PROBLEM
● It is quite difficult to avoid planetary movement unless you have some exceptionally heavy duty lifting gear

LOOK ON THE BRIGHT SIDE
● We'll get a really good view of Mercury... for a few seconds

"That's a relief...I thought you were a salesman."

HOW TO AVOID THE PROBLEM
- Start living as a hermit (and if you survive there will be no other option)
- Consider closing down your rat emporium and flea circus

LOOK ON THE BRIGHT SIDE
- It will be boom time again in the bring-out-your-dead business

50

BUBONIC PLAGUE

Bubonic plague was big news during the Middle Ages but doesn't seem to have bothered us too much in recent years. Or has it? Things from medieval times can often make unexpected and unwelcome comebacks as Sting demonstrated when he released that album of lute music.

In 1348 Italy's biggest export to the rest of Europe wasn't tomato puree, pasta or miniature plastic models of the pope. Instead it was the rather less appreciated Black Death. Bubonic plague had arrived in Sicily in October 1347 at the end of a trade route from China and from there it went on to its famous mid-century tour of Europe. By 1349 it had reached England where it killed 1.5 million people out of a population of four million which meant that every single person left alive could be usefully employed in the grave digging business. Across Europe as a whole the plague is believed to have killed between 25 and 50 million.

Lumps or buboes in the armpits or groin were the first sign of the disease followed by black spots on the arms and thighs. Boccaccio recorded that few recovered and that almost all died within three days. Some extremely lucky souls did however manage to hang on for four.

Until the 17th century the plague kept coming back every few years like an unwanted fashion trend. Today you might think that the plague is all over and done with if it wasn't for the fact that the most recent resurgence of the plague was considered active until 1959! Clearly our newspapers miss the occasional major story. This Asian bubonic plague killed an estimated 12 million in India and China in the late nineteenth and early twentieth century.

Even today there are around 2,000 cases of bubonic plague recorded every year. If the plague killed the same proportion of people around the world as it did in Europe in the Middle Ages 2.2 billion people would die and the life insurance industry would be in significant trouble.

The only bubonic plague vaccine in existence works for only half of the people to whom it is given to and which half is unclear. The thing that might help the plague go on another round the world comeback tour is a series of wet humid summers.

So there's another boon from global warming for us!

TELLTALE SIGNS IT'S HAPPENING
- Buboes under your arm or around your groin
- Everyone will know what a buboe is

WHERE NOT TO STAND
- Near any over-detailed Medieval re-enactments
- Too close to the edge of any large pits dug for plague victims

51

HOW TO AVOID THE PROBLEM
- Factor 50 trillion sun cream might do the trick

LOOK ON THE BRIGHT SIDE
- It might give you a lovely all over even tan just before you get frazzled

COSMIC RADIATION

If someone bursts a paper bag, it can give you a nasty start. So just imagine the effects of a supernova explosion carrying all the energy our sun will produce over its entire ten billion year lifespan. If one of these occurs at a distance of one light year from Earth, not only will we all suddenly die, we'll all do so with extremely surprised expressions on our faces.

When large stars reach the end of their life and finally run out of pop, they can suffer devastating core collapse and explode. We've all had days like that, haven't we? A collapsing massive star explodes as a supernova which can burn as bright as an entire galaxy. The cosmic rays the supernova throws out could suddenly and unexpectedly hit us and threaten life on Earth.

Supernovae occur about once every 50 years in our galaxy which seems to give us some sort of fighting chance. Unfortunately in the universe as a whole a supernova occurs once every second! OK, we're a safe distance from most of them but supernova explosions launch cosmic rays including gamma rays across the universe. If these hit us they could destroy the ozone layer and so let in the sun's ultra violet rays. This would have a catastrophic effect on life on Earth although on the plus side we wouldn't need to worry about the effects of CFCs any more. The rays would also come from one direction across space and would therefore only hit one side of the Earth at a time. This should give us all a 50/50 chance of survival depending on where we're standing at the time.

Unfortunately we would then find one of two things. Either every one on the other side of the planet had unexpectedly died or the cosmic rays from outer space would have transformed half the world's population into superheroes like the Incredible Hulk or the Fantastic Four leaving the rest of us feeling slightly inadequate.

TELLTALE SIGNS IT'S HAPPENING
- Everyone on one side of the world will die
- Everyone on the other side of the world will be saying, "Where's everyone else gone?"

WHERE NOT TO STAND
- In any patches of oddly glowing light

DECLINE OF FERTILITY

Human beings have existed for hundreds of thousands of years. In recent years however there has been a dramatic decline in human fertility. Well, you know how it is when you've been with the same partner for a long time...

The recent worrying decline in human fertility can be blamed on a number of factors. These include lifestyle and pollutants in the atmosphere but the most likely cause must be the state of the alcohol industry. As we all know previous generations relied on the effects of copious amounts of alcohol to assist in reproducing the species. This has however had a terrible effect. It has allowed the surival of a number of very ugly people who would otherwise have been removed from the gene pool by means of natural selection. This means the human race is getting uglier and uglier and in a few generations we will all require cosmetic surgery immediately after being born.

The fate of humanity has therefore been placed in the hands of brewers and their ability to come up with stronger and stronger types of alcohol. Nevertheless the ratio between how ugly a person can be and how drunk their partner can get without completely passing out must ultimately reach a critical tipping point which will prove disastrous for the future of humanity.

At the same time as facing catastrophe due to declining fertility, we are also facing cataclysm because of massive overpopulation. This makes the situation even more desperate because in a few years there will be several billion more of us and we'll all be suffering from fertility problems.

TELLTALE SIGNS IT'S HAPPENING
• Human pregnancy will become a newsworthy event

WHERE NOT TO STAND
• Near anyone who has become noticeably sexually desperate

HOW TO AVOID THE PROBLEM
- Be fruitful and multiply
- If you can't manage that, just eat the fruit
- Clone yourself (which will also help you see what the rest of us have put up with all these years)

LOOK ON THE BRIGHT SIDE
- No more worries about accidental pregnancy
- No more annoying kids anywhere!

LITTLE (FARM) SHOP OF HORRORS

G.M CROP NOW IN !

mosedale

HOW TO AVOID THE PROBLEM
- You could try developing a genetically modified parasite
- Eat everything in sight

LOOK ON THE BRIGHT SIDE
- You won't go hungry

GENETICALLY MODIFIED CROPS TAKE OVER THE WORLD

They are called Frankenstein foods but so far there have been few if any reported cases of people being picked up and throttled by a ten-foot high tomato with a bolt through its neck.

The notion of Frankenstein foods clearly led a lot of people to assume that scientists were attempting to transplant the brains of insane murderers into radishes. Some even suggested that the choice of the term Frankenstein foods was a poor one for scientists to have chosen as their marketing angle. In fact naming them Frankenstein foods was a brilliant strategy to get young children to eat their vegetables by tricking them into believing they were scoffing something a bit like Monster Munch.

Very few small boys would willingly consume a plate of spinach, cabbage and broccoli. Tell them they've got "Frankenstein food" for dinner tonight though and they won't be able to get enough of the stuff inside them. And not only does this get children to eat their greens, it also provides scientists with a readily available supply of willing guinea pigs on whom they can test their culinary experiments for any appalling side effects.

The worry is that genetically modifying crops to make them drought and pest resistant could also make them dangerous to eat. This would particularly be the case for anyone who consumes them while already in a weakened state for example because they are among the 12.5% of the world's population who currently don't get enough to eat.

It is also believed that if scientists produce completely pest resistant crops these will grow everywhere. A vast swathe of horrifying genetically modified wheat will cover every inch of the Earth and obliterate all of mankind.

There will be nothing any of us can do but stand in horror before its horrifying advance. It should also be noted that there is no truth whatsoever in the rumour that Elton John once offered his scalp as a possible GM crop test site.

TELLTALE SIGNS IT'S HAPPENING
- GM crops will be growing anywhere and everywhere

WHERE NOT TO STAND
- Near any unstably propped up giant vegetables

57

HIV

The 1980s were famous for many fads that we would rather not remember. The New Romantic movement was one, AIDS was another. Worrying advertisements appeared warning that we would all die of ignorance and it was important to wear a condom at all times even if you were just going to the shops.

Because of its initial association with the gay community, many kindly God loving folk decreed that AIDS was divine retribution on them. This was despite the fact that this would mean that all epidemics were also punishment. The Black Death must therefore have been sent to punish people in the Middle Ages for having invented the madrigal.

In recent years it may seem as though AIDS is less of a problem than it once was. This may be because people have started using the term "advanced HIV" instead of AIDS. There are however no plans to re-launch the early 1980s slimming biscuits called Ayds.

In fact the number of people with HIV has more than quadrupled since 1990. By the end of 2007, 33,000,000 people were infected around the world with about 2,500,000 becoming newly infected every year. In other words that's about one every 15 seconds.

If, as it seems, Mother Nature is keen to wipe us all out, sexually transmitted diseases are a good method to use. After all without sex none of us would be here at all and most glossy magazines would be full of completely blank pages.

Clearly, as in the 1980s, the only way for humanity to survive is for us all to wear condoms at all times. Ironically though, this will also of course quickly lead to the end of the human race.

TELLTALE SIGNS IT'S HAPPENING
- The people who liked to blame it on gay people and drug addicts will have fallen oddly silent
- Everyone you meet will suddenly be working to find a cure

WHERE NOT TO STAND
- Completely inside a condom. It gets quite difficult to breathe

HOW TO AVOID THE PROBLEM
• Stop having sex

LOOK ON THE BRIGHT SIDE
• No more sex for anyone – it'll be just like being married

"If it's sympathy you're after... forget it!"

HOW TO AVOID THE PROBLEM
• For you as a human avoiding the extinction of the human species might be tricky
• You could try inter-marrying with another ape species

LOOK ON THE BRIGHT SIDE
• It could solve so many of the world's other problems at a stroke

HUMAN EXTINCTION

Human extinction: the end of the world scenario that every other animal on Earth would probably vote for. But with over 6.6 billion people currently on the planet it seems highly unlikely that the human race could become extinct. On the other hand some of us are extremely ugly...

More than 99.9% of the species that have ever existed on Earth are now extinct. As we've seen we humans are currently working hard to try and get this up to a nice round figure. Surprisingly though, of all the species who have become extinct, only 4% disappeared in a cataclysmic blowout like the dinosaurs. The rest seem to have just quietly collected their coats and slipped away. Obviously after a few hundred thousand years the spark had gone and they just couldn't be bothered making the effort to keep their species going.

One theory suggests that the same thing could happen to humans. It's not just individual humans that get old, it's the entire species. On the end of each living creature's chromosomes are protective caps called telomeres. During an individual's lifetime cells divide and are copied. As the individual gets older the copying gets less perfect but calling in the service engineer from Rank Xerox isn't an option.

Over the years this increasingly poor quality copying results in the individual's telomeres getting shorter and shorter and age related illnesses such as heart attacks, Alzheimer's disease and cancer can begin to occur.

According to the theory not only do these telomeres get shorter during an individual's lifetime but they also slowly get shorter from generation to generation of an entire species. Once they become too short the species becomes extinct.

So not only could this spell the end for human kind, it's like finding each of us has got an expiry date printed somewhere about our person.

TELLTALE SIGNS IT'S HAPPENING

- You'll spot be able to tell that it's happened because you won't be here to notice
- You will be extinct
- If you're anywhere you might find yourself as an exhibit in a natural history museum

WHERE NOT TO STAND

- Anywhere near any of the last surviving humans desperate to try and preserve the species

MEGA-TSUNAMI

A mega-tsunami is a tsunami but one that is really mega! It is clear that scientists worked with great sensitivity to come up with a name for this phenomenon that could cause destruction and loss of life on an extraordinary scale. They considered calling it the super tsunami, the jumbo tsunami and the tsunami whopper before finally settling on mega-tsunami.

If you drop a small stone into some water it will cause a small splash. Building up from this simple idea, scientists have wondered about chucking half an island into the Atlantic to see what would happen. The answer is a tidal wave 160 feet (50 m) high which would travel across the ocean and destroy the eastern side of the United States. And unfortunately this could actually happen.

A volcano on the island of La Palma in the Canary Islands erupted in 1949. When it did so, it developed a huge split down one side. And that's bad enough when it happens to a supermarket carrier bag. The western side of the volcano moved towards the ocean but then decided to pause before plunging in. Nearly 50 years later, it's still thinking about it probably because seawater can be quite nippy when you first get in.

The only way to stop La Palma cracking further is to daub the entire island in large quantities of L'Oreal Age Re-Perfect. Well, if it worked for Jane Fonda it could work for a large million year old lump of cracked volcanic rock in the middle of the Atlantic.

Meantime it has been calculated that around 500 trillion tonnes of rock is due to fall off La Palma into the Atlantic at any point in the next few thousand years. The resulting tidal wave would hit Boston first before devastating the entire East coast of the USA all the way down to Florida and the Caribbean. The wave would plunge 13 miles (20 km) inland meaning that it would for the first time literally be possible to go surfing across the USA.

Some authorities have played down the possibility of a mega-tsunami occurring. Among these has been the government of the Canary Islands. After all you know what the USA is like for taking pre-emptive action against anyone threatening it.

TELLTALE SIGNS IT'S HAPPENING
- Fifty foot high wall of water heading straight towards your house
- Catastrophic destruction of big swathes of land
- You will get a bit wet

WHERE NOT TO STAND
- Immediately in front of the wave pointing and saying, "Hey, everyone! Look at this really big wave."
- On top of the wave attempting to surf

HOW TO AVOID THE PROBLEM

• Hide behind a large sand bag – one about 161 feet high should do the trick

LOOK ON THE BRIGHT SIDE

• Who knows! Having that amount of water land on top of you might be quite refreshing

"Admit it... we're bloody well lost!"

HOW TO AVOID THE PROBLEM
• Look in a mirror everywhere you go and things should be the right way round again

LOOK ON THE BRIGHT SIDE
• You never knew which way you were going before anyway

POLAR SHIFT

According to some scientists the Earth's magnetic field could flip over at any time. This will have disastrous consequences for the climate, for animal migration and for any boy scouts trying to get their compass reading badges.

The Earth is an enormous magnet. Examination of its magnetic field has however shown that it has decayed by 5% in the last 150 years. Eventually it could decay to nothing at all. You will know when this happens because anything made of iron will start to float off into space. This means that whenever you park your car not only will you have to put on the handbrake, you'll also have to anchor it to the road.

Reasons given for the failing of the Earth's magnetic field include the movement of molten iron beneath the planet's surface. Or it could be that we forgot to put a magnet protector across the planet when we put it back in the drawer in the school physics laboratory.

Eventually the Earth's magnetic field may come back as though someone has been trying to fix it by switching it off and then switching it back on again. When it comes back however we may discover that the north and south poles are the wrong way round. No, seriously!

It is believed that on average the poles pull this swapping-round-with-each-other stunt every 250,000 years. The last reversal was 780,000 years ago. So we're definitely due for another. The loss of the Earth's magnetic field could in itself easily lead to the end of humanity. Firstly the field helps protect us from harmful solar radiation and secondly the loss of the field will play havoc with animal migration patterns. So if any of us survive the radiation we will then be knocked out by the millions of confused birds who have been flying round in circles until they got dizzy and fell out of the sky.

It will however all be good news for explorers like Sir Ranulph Fiennes who will surely be keen to become the first person to walk backwards to the North Pole now it's the South Pole.

TELLTALE SIGNS IT'S HAPPENING
- Birds will start flying North for the winter
- You will start to hear the phrase "it's grim up south"

WHERE NOT TO STAND
- Immediately underneath any confused migrating birds

BLACK HOLES

There is only one thing worse that being stretched out and torn apart as you are sucked inside a black hole and that is being stretched out and torn apart as you are sucked inside a black hole while Stephen Hawking excitedly tells you, "Isn't this great? It's exactly as I predicted!"

There are so many black holes in the universe it is impossible to count them. Black holes are so powerful they suck everything into themselves and nothing can ever escape. Surely the Earth must be destined to one day disappear down one of these vast astronomical plug holes like an unwanted cosmic toenail.

Black holes are formed by objects in space that have so much mass in such a small space nothing can escape their gravitational pull – not even light. Black holes will eat stars, planets and just about anything. This means the area of space around them will be quite empty apart from an occasional gherkin that they've left on one side.

If you fall into a black hole the theory is you will be stretched to incredible length. If you want to use your new found slimmer figure to pursue a career as a supermodel, you'll have to be quick because you will simultaneously be heated to millions of degrees before being swallowed.

There is a black hole at the centre of our very own Milky Way galaxy that has swallowed as much material as four million suns. Scientists also believe that there may be hundreds of rogue black holes each of which is several thousand times bigger than our sun wandering around the galaxy. This sounds as though we could bump into a black hole just about anywhere but apparently we are fairly safe from being swallowed.

The real danger of black holes is that a decent sized one might pass by the outer regions of our solar system and cause a hail of comets to fire at us. So they might kill us but they probably won't eat us which is somehow vaguely insulting.

TELLTALE SIGNS IT'S HAPPENING

- A large hole will be consuming you and everything else you can see
- You will be stretched out to enormous length
- Stephen Hawking will get excited

WHERE NOT TO STAND

- With your head sticking inside the black hole so you can get a good look

"It appeared last week, so we've extended the course."

HOW TO AVOID THE PROBLEM
• Try coating yourself all over with Tabasco in the hope that the hole will spit you out

LOOK ON THE BRIGHT SIDE
• You always wanted to be thinner and taller

HOW TO AVOID THE PROBLEM
• As long as your life ends some time within the next 50 billion years you should be OK

LOOK ON THE BRIGHT SIDE
• Is there a bright side to the end of the entire universe?
• There might be a big send off party

BIG CRUNCH

The Big Crunch, the Big Rip and the Big Bounce have all been suggested as possible ends to our universe that began with the Big Bang. The idea of crunching, ripping and bouncing does however make it sound as though the universe is destined to end in a moment of cosmic slapstick or cackhandedness. Scientists are indeed working to combine the three concepts into a single end of the universe scenario called the Big Oh Bugger I've Just Dropped The Bloody Thing.

In the Big Crunch the universe will reach a point of extreme expansion following the Big Bang before starting to collapse back in on itself. The whole of time will therefore starting running backwards which will be particularly bad news as it will mean that flared trousers will come back into fashion at least twice more. During this process all matter will eventually collapse into black holes, which is why the universe will end with the Big Crunch followed a few moments later by the Cosmic Belch. The Big Bounce will involve the entire universe repeatedly inflating and shrinking like a middle-aged person undergoing an extreme diet regime.

The Big Rip now seems the most likely end to everything. It involves all matter in the universe being torn apart. This will either be because of the expansion of the universe or because in 20 billion years' time we will have accumulated so much junk mail there will be no choice but to put the entire universe into a vast shredder in a final effort to protect ourselves from identity theft.

These events are not due to happen for a little while although we will know if time does start running backwards because we will start passing ourselves everywhere we go.

If the universe does end by any one of these processes it should not happen for several billion years. This means that if you place a bet on the correct outcome now your winnings could be immense. Admittedly though you will have very little time to spend them.

TELLTALE SIGNS IT'S HAPPENING
- The universe will start collapsing around you

WHERE NOT TO STAND
- Anywhere in the universe

GALAXY COLLISION

Getting caught in a hailstone shower can be quite painful. So getting caught in a sudden downpour that comprises the trillion suns of the Andromeda galaxy is definitely going to smart.

Space was given its name (i.e. space) for quite a good reason. It's extraordinarily big and if there's one thing it's not short of, it's space. So given the amount of space in space you would think it unlikely that galaxies would ever run into each other even if one of them happened to be distracted for a moment by the sight of another very attractive galaxy on the other side of the road.

Galaxy collision is however quite common in the evolution of galaxies. Our own Milky Way galaxy has itself eaten a number of other smaller galaxies in its time which it has naturally managed to do between meals without ruining its appetite.

The Milky Way and the Andromeda galaxy are the largest members of our local group of about 40 galaxies. Unfortunately Andromeda and Milky Way are rushing in each other's general direction right now like two great galaxy-sized clumsy oafs. And if you race towards anything at 75 miles per second it's surely going to lead to trouble.

A merger between Andromeda and the Milky Way will therefore surely occur at some point and when it does large scale redundancies can't be ruled out.

The collision and the galaxy-sized game of pinball that will follow are not however due to take place for about five billion years. Even so, immediately afterwards, we will all no doubt be saying, "What was that? It all seemed to happen so fast."

TELLTALE SIGNS IT'S HAPPENING
- Conditions of cataclysmic catastrophe

WHERE NOT TO STAND
- Avoiding each of the colliding galaxies might be best

HOW TO AVOID THE PROBLEM
• If you can't get out of the way of the colliding galaxies in time try sitting in your car in the hope that your airbag will cushion the blow

LOOK ON THE BRIGHT SIDE
• The newly merged super galaxy could adopt one of those heart warming slogans like, "Together we're stronger!"

HOW TO AVOID THE PROBLEM
● Build a very big snowman

LOOK ON THE BRIGHT SIDE
● It will be like Christmas every single day – for 250 million years!

ICE AGE

We could soon be plunged into a new ice age. This will be unfortunate because we're just not dressed for it.

The arrival of a new ice age will cause catastrophe and bring our society to its knees. In fact our society tends to be brought to its knees every time we get a slightly heavier than expected snow shower. So goodness knows what a new ice age will do.

There have been four major ice ages in the Earth's history. One lasted 250 million years, the next 30 million years and another went on for 90 million years. The most recent ice age only started 2.58 million years ago. This means either it was a very short ice age or that it hasn't really gone away but is just hiding somewhere.

We could therefore still be in the middle of an ice age which could explain why your partner's feet never seem to warm up in bed at night.

If the ice age returns not only will we find it hard to survive but it will be incredibly difficult to stand up without slipping over. We are of course also facing the problem of global warming. You will notice if we get hit by global warming at the same time as an ice age because all the ice will be warmer and a bit more liquidy than normal and this will make it quite difficult to walk on.

It is therefore feasible that the disaster of global warming could combine with the nightmare of an ice age and create an ultimate catastrophe in which conditions end up exactly the same as they started out.

TELLTALE SIGNS IT'S HAPPENING

- When you look out of your window you will see an expanse of icy wasteland
- You might have to turn the central heating up
- It'll be a bit nippy out

WHERE NOT TO STAND

- In the middle of the icy wasteland in just your underpants

EXPLOSION OF THE SUN

Some people like to call themselves sun lovers. Let's see how much they love it when they're standing in it.

Gravity becomes an increasing problem for lots of us as we get older. Not only do we find it more difficult to get upstairs but our back, breasts and genitals seem increasingly drawn towards the ground.

The effects of gravity on our ageing sun will be slightly more troubling. Its centre will begin to collapse and it will completely destroy the Earth.

The sun is believed to be in the middle of its life. It has settled down, it has its little family of planets around it and it is considered fairly unremarkable compared to its fellow stars. Each day it keeps itself busy with its regular job as a star which, in its case, is squeezing hydrogen nuclei by means of its enormous gravitational force until they turn into helium.

The sun is in fact getting through 700,000,000 tons of hydrogen every second and has been doing so for the past 4.5 billion years. This is one hell of an addiction. Unsurprisingly it can't carry on like this forever. And when it runs out of fuel it will quite literally come running to us.

The sun's core will contract and its outer layers will expand until it is perhaps 250 times its current size. This means it will reach you wherever you are on this planet even if you live at the end of a really long road.

Luckily the sun has a billion billion billion tons of matter so it can afford to be a bit profligate with its hydrogen supply. So it shouldn't actually arrive at your door for another four billion years. If however you ever notice some ashen faced scientists muttering about getting their calculations wrong while rubbing factor one trillion sun lotion over each other, start worrying!

TELLTALE SIGNS IT'S HAPPENING

- The sun will be exploding
- Everyone will be talking about the fact that the sun is exploding
- The sun will reach as far as our planet although it will still be slightly overcast in parts of Scotland

WHERE NOT TO STAND

- Right in the middle of the sun

"Right, two billion years is up. Don't know about you but I'm packing up."

HOW TO AVOID THE PROBLEM
- Stand in the shade
- If you see the sun suddenly inflating until it fills the sky wrap yourself in a fire blanket

LOOK ON THE BRIGHT SIDE
- You won't need a jumper

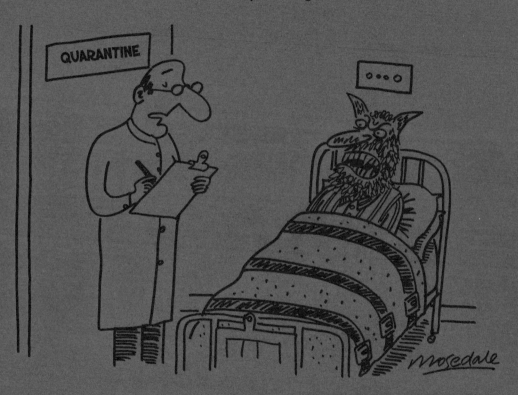

"You seem rather ungrateful Mr. Jenkins. This new drug means you'll never have hayfever again."

HOW TO AVOID THE PROBLEM
• Develop your own artificially created disease and then your own artificially created antidote

LOOK ON THE BRIGHT SIDE
• It will give old people some interesting new diseases to moan to each other about

76

ARTIFICIALLY CREATED DISEASES

Over the centuries people have wished for many strange things and yet no-one has ever said, "Do you know what? I really wish there were a few more terrible deadly diseases in the world." Nevertheless the internet has now seen fit to cater for this particular specialized market...

People use the internet to create all kinds of things. Some use it to put together their own compilation CDs, others to assemble the air travel, accommodation and quarantine programme for their holiday, others to build up a definitive catalogue of pictures of Britney Spears bending over. Meanwhile others show similar levels of creativity in using the internet to assemble the elements required to create brand new diseases. Yes, there are people out there who think that the thing the world really needs is an all new version of the Ebola virus.

It is literally possible to buy the elements you need to create your own diseases such as pieces of viral DNA. A number of companies exist offering commercial gene synthesis. So if you are a creatively minded yet evil chemist with internet access you can brew up your very own anthrax for the 21st century or create a new improved re-mix of the 1918 flu pandemic.

So just why do people feel the need to create their own diseases? Is there someone somewhere who owns the copyright on the existing diseases? Are people worried that if they launch a pandemic they will be charged a royalty for every million who get struck down?

On the other hand if they launch a new disease to strike down the world's population just wait until the compensation culture begins to kick in.

TELLTALE SIGNS IT'S HAPPENING

- People will start dying in new and unexpected ways
- People will start dying in new and unexpected quantities
- Doctors will frequently use expressions such as, "I've not seen anything like this before" and, "This is the tenth case of this I've seen this morning"

WHERE NOT TO STAND

- Among other human beings
- In the middle of any clouds of artificially created virus you find hanging around

BIOLOGICAL WEAPONS

As one expert says, it has never been easier to develop biological weapons – all you need to do is look on the internet! Not only that but they're attractive to terrorists because they're cheap to produce. So they're ideal for the would-be mass murderer on a budget!

There are at least 30 different microbes that could be used as biological weapons. These include Ricin, Smallpox, Plague and Anthrax. These are also four of the least popular flavours for crisps ever invented.

The biological terrorist mass murderer's weapon of choice is anthrax. Anthrax is a naturally occurring substance first discovered by the ancient Egyptians in 1500 BC and particularly found in animals such as sheep. For similar reasons early biological warfare consisted of simply lobbing an entire diseased animal carcass over the castle walls at your enemies. When launched into the air as a biological weapon, anthrax spores are quite deadly and will kill nine out of ten people who breathe them into their lungs. Anthrax is not however contagious although this could of course be due to the fact that it doesn't leave anyone alive long enough to pass it on.

Anthrax therefore seems ideal for terrorists wanting to commit mass murder and destroy civilization except for one thing: you've got to get all your potential victims to stand in one place in favourable weather conditions. People are usually unwilling to do this particularly when they discover the object of the exercise is to sprinkle them with anthrax. The group that used nerve gas to kill 12 people on the Tokyo subway in 1995 had made at least eight previous unsuccessful anthrax attacks. This shows that anthrax is simultaneously both a deadly threat to humanity and a bit rubbish.

The British cannot take the high moral ground on anthrax as they worked to develop biological weapons during WWII. They looked around for somewhere they could test anthrax without threatening civilization. In the end they decided to use an island a couple of miles off Scotland.

Gruinard Island remained contaminated with anthrax from 1942 to 1990 when it was deemed safe after being washed with formaldehyde. Sheep have lived on the island ever since without any problem apart from an allergic reaction to formaldehyde. It is not clear however if lamb marked as "fresh from Gruinard Island" is a strong marketing angle. Hang on though – wasn't it sheep that anthrax came from in the first place?

TELLTALE SIGNS IT'S HAPPENING
- Mass terror/ Mass death
- Biological protection suits will suddenly become very fashionable

WHERE NOT TO STAND
- Anywhere inside the Anthrax sufferers' isolation ward at the local hospital

"My wife misread the invite and packed the wrong suit."

BIOLOGICAL
WEAPONS
CONVENTION

HOW TO AVOID THE PROBLEM
• Wear a biological protection suit all day
• At night wear biological protection pyjamas

LOOK ON THE BRIGHT SIDE
• It should make your local town centre a bit less busy

HOW TO AVOID THE PROBLEM
- Be nice to any ecosystems you come across

LOOK ON THE BRIGHT SIDE
- The environment! Pah! Who needs it!

COLLAPSE OF ECOSYSTEMS

The term ecosystem was coined in 1930 by British botanist Roy "Ecosystem" Clapham. This was ironic as Clapham itself is one of the few places on earth not to have an ecosystem.

An ecosystem is defined as being an environmental system full of living creatures all of whom are in some sort of relationship with every one of their fellows. By this definition television soap operas are ecosystems because all the characters in them have had relationships with all the others at some stage. More specifically an ecosystem is all the animals, insects, bacteria, plants, mosses and other gunky stuff that live together in one area and which all feed off each other. So there's probably an ecosystem down the back of your fridge.

Our world is made up of a series of vast eco-systems that are naturally capable of constantly evolving and supporting life. At least they were until we came along. According to a 2006 WWF report, we are using 25% more resources than we renew and there has been a 30% decline in species in terrestrial, marine and freshwater eco-systems. The amount we need to sustain our current lifestyles is so great we need three planets rather than one to support us. So by 2050 the world's ecosystem should collapse completely and we will realize that endless growth isn't possible no matter what all those adverts for penis enlargement say.

From childhood we have been unable to resist taking our toys apart and then seeing if we can put them back together. Now we're doing exactly the same thing with the world's ecosystems. Unfortunately no-ne in history has ever managed to take something apart and successfully put it back together again.

What the effect of the collapse of an entire ecosystem will be like is unclear although it will probably be followed by a drunken cheer from one part of the crowd.

TELLTALE SIGNS IT'S HAPPENING
- Total environmental disaster

WHERE NOT TO STAND
- In the environment

COMPUTERS TAKE OVER THE WORLD

There is some debate about the year in which computers will become more intelligent than people and so gain mastery of the planet. Some say it will happen in 2028. Others maintain that many of us were surpassed in ability and intelligence several years ago with the invention of the Corby Trouser Press.

We sit shouting and cursing at our PCs because they have failed to understand what we want them to do. Surely that's eventually going to make them cross. What's more, computers have for decades been growing increasingly powerful, intelligent and compact.

In other words they've been doing exactly the opposite of us.

Moore's Law was propounded in 1965 by Gordon E Moore, the co-founder of Intel. This should have said that you will know when computers have taken over the world because every time you hear the word "Intel" you will hear a little jingle play inside your head. What it in fact predicted was that the number of transistors you could fit on a computer chip would double every two years.

Computers have indeed been doubling in capability about every 24 months. We, on the other hand, are getting increasingly stupid because every 24 months it becomes slightly easier to get computers to do anything that requires any real mental effort.

The day will soon come when the most intelligent things on the planet are not humans but computers. Already computers have drawn millions into subservience by their crafty provision of an infinite number of porn sites and order-on-line pizza delivery services. Clearly the computers are recruiting an army of geek drones who will serve them, do their constant bidding and switch them off and then on again if they ever go wrong.

Stephen Hawking has said that humans should start genetically modifying themselves to keep ahead of the advances in computer and robot technology.

If you can't beat them, then simply re-engineer yourself to become part human being part android like The Terminator or former British Prime Minister Tony Blair.

TELLTALE SIGNS IT'S HAPPENING
- Your computer will start telling you what to do if it hasn't already
- You will notice your computer moving around the house on its little trolley pretending to be a dalek

WHERE NOT TO STAND
- In front of any advancing computer army

82

HOW TO AVOID THE PROBLEM
- Get yourself converted to be half human half computer
- Unplug the bastards!

LOOK ON THE BRIGHT SIDE
- They're bound to make a better job of running the world than we did

FOOTBALL
RESULTS
LIV 1   EV 2
MUFD 4   LUFD 0

HOW TO AVOID THE PROBLEM
• Try using your brain and your body occasionally, perhaps on alternate days

LOOK ON THE BRIGHT SIDE
• Life will be a lot simpler when we've all de-evolved

DE-EVOLUTION

Human evolution is about to go into reverse. Eventually we will turn into puny creatures with wasted limbs who are seemingly incapable of doing anything useful. So if you want to know what the future holds for humanity, Victoria Beckham might give you some sort of idea (legal note: – this is because she is a well known expert on the subject).

The concept of de-evolution is based on the idea that humanity will attain a peak level of development and then start going into decline or de-evolving. A look around at your fellow humans might lead to the conclusion that some of them have started early.

In fact it's not possible to de-evolve as such. Despite the apparent evidence suggested by ex-president George W. Bush, we're not about to turn back into a race of chimpanzees. The possibility must exist however that the human race will adapt physically and mentally to changing circumstances. No-one likes doing hard physical work. For this reason we have created various machines to perform these unpleasant manual tasks for us. This means that there isn't so much need for us all to have the perfect bodies and great rippling muscles we currently possess. Because there is no need for us to be physically strong, our bodies may slowly degenerate until they are barely capable of holding up our heads and the massive bulging brains contained therein.

There's just one thing. We've also created a range of machines to perform any difficult mental tasks for us because we weren't very keen on doing those either.

Eventually therefore humans could evolve to be both very weak and very stupid. So the future will not be one in which we possess brains like Stephen Hawking and bodies likes great sportsmen. Unfortunately it will be the other way round.

The end of human civilization will therefore come about with us all evolving into vegetables. Or, to be more precise, couch potatoes.

TELLTALE SIGNS IT'S HAPPENING

- You will get progressively stupider and weaker
- You could find yourself turning back into an unmuscular Neanderthal Man and not a very pretty one at that
- You will become so dim you will ironically stop believing in the concept of evolution

WHERE NOT TO STAND

- Don't worry, you'll be too weak to stand

85

NUCLEAR WAR

Nuclear war is an end-of-the-world classic. It's a thermonuclear blast from the past that could be heading for a re-release some time very soon.

A few years ago nuclear war was the odds on favourite end of the world scenario. The world was surely going to end in horrific nuclear war. This would either follow a breakdown in relations between the USA and the Soviet Union or someone one day saying, "Hey! Does anyone know what this button here does?" If you are hit by a nuclear explosion you will know about it. If you're lucky, you won't know about it for long.

There will be an initial blast not unlike that from a conventional bomb except for the fact that it is millions of times stronger. There will also be a sudden rise in temperature to several million degrees. So if that doesn't make you sit up and pay attention nothing will.

Then of course there is the radioactive damage which can burn and temporarily blind you and cause major damage to your bone marrow, central nervous system, skin, intestines, cataracts and lungs which are all things that you ideally wouldn't want to do without.

Nuclear bombs also lead to widespread radioactive fallout and contamination. This makes them unlikely to win any awards for being environmentally friendly. Nevertheless the fact that they kill tens of thousands in one go presumably saves something in terms of transportation and packaging costs.

Nuclear warfare would therefore be a quick and efficient way to place the entire planet beyond further possible use. Despite this the superpowers during the cold war kept building their nuclear arsenals until they were able to destroy the planet and several times over. Presumably this was in case they missed on the first attempt.

Many say that the world was saved from conflict during the cold war because the superpowers realized the apocalyptic consequences of a nuclear war. Now all we need is for nuclear weapons to fall into the hands of those who aren't such big cissies. This may indeed happen as it becomes easier to acquire nuclear material from the former Soviet Union via Ebay or a car boot sale.

Disaster will then surely follow...

TELLTALE SIGNS IT'S HAPPENING
- Mushroom cloud on the horizon
- Sudden unseasonal rise in temperature to 300,000° C
- Nuclear winter
- Membership boom for CND

WHERE NOT TO STAND
- Avoiding the blast zone would be sensible

"Now look what you've done."

HOW TO AVOID THE PROBLEM
- Nuclear bunker
- Paper bag on the head was once recommended

LOOK ON THE BRIGHT SIDE
- Another opportunity to develop superhuman powers

HOW TO AVOID THE PROBLEM
- Get hold of the remote control for these nano robots and switch them off
- Try and avoid being eaten by disguising yourself as something inedible like quinoa

LOOK ON THE BRIGHT SIDE
- Grey goes with most things

GREY GOO

In the near future microscopic nano-robots will run out of control and eat anything and everything until all that is left of us and our planet is a great porridgey mess or "grey goo". The only things that seem less than certain are the exact shade of grey and the exact consistency of the goo.

The "grey goo" idea was dreamed up as a worst case scenario in Eric Drexler's 1986 book *Engines of Creation: The Coming Era of Nanotechnology.* The book described what would happen if nanotechnology were developed and then got out of control. The good news is that since the book was published nanotechnology has indeed come on in leaps and bounds! Nanotechnology will involve the widespread use of nanobots. A nanobot is not as you might think an android grandmother but a robot so small it has to be measured on the nano scale. The nano scale is quite a small scale. A human hair for example would be 10,000 nanometres thick or, in Ross Kemp's case, long.

These atom-sized C3P0s would exist to provide incredible new ways of manufacturing and fixing things. They would also be used in the sorts of medical procedures for which we once envisaged shrinking Raquel Welch down to microscopic size.

The nanobots would be capable of sensing and learning about the world around them, they would be able to consume whatever they needed to keep themselves going and they could build more and more of themselves as they saw necessary.

Can you spot the snag in the idea? It's somewhere in the "consuming whatever they need to keep going" and the "building more and more of themselves as they see necessary" parts of the equation.

The nanobots will eventually think, "Oh stuff all this manufacturing and fixing stuff! Let's just carry on eating and making more and more ourselves." In other words these plagues of millions of tiny robotic insects will start behaving exactly like us humans.

Then we really would be in the brown stuff or, more accurately the "grey goo".

TELLTALE SIGNS IT'S HAPPENING

• You and everything else will have been eaten by nano robots

• There will be nothing left of the planet except "grey goo"

WHERE NOT TO STAND

• In the "grey goo" – unfortunately though this will be the only place to stand

E-BOMB

An E-bomb is a bomb that wouldn't kill a single person or damage a single building. Despite this it would, in an instant, destroy our entire civilization. On the plus side it is the one bomb that leaves everything nice and tidy...

It would be terrible if computers ever took over the world and made us their slaves. In fact there could only be one thing worse: if every computer in the world suddenly broke down and the horrible realization suddenly hit us that we have in fact been completely dependent on computers for some years already. And that's what would happen if someone exploded an E-bomb.

An E-bomb is not, as many believe, an online auction site where you can buy and sell weapons of mass destruction but a device that produces an EMP or electromagnetic pulse when it explodes.

An EMP will kill stone dead any electronic systems including integrated circuits caught in its blast. It will cause more computers to break down than a pensioner visiting his local library to do a spot of on-line research.

Not only will all computers suddenly die but so too will anything remotely computerized. TVs, ovens, power supplies, water supplies, hospitals, cars, trains, aeroplanes, air traffic control and Stephen Hawking's wheelchair will all stop working in an instant. If you've been fitted with a pacemaker you better watch out as well.

The EMP could come from an electro-magnetic bomb or it could be produced by a good old fashioned nuclear device. It is believed that a 1.4 megaton bomb exploded 250 miles above Kansas would destroy almost every single piece of electronic equipment in the USA. This would then cause Microsoft's telephone help desk staff to be swamped with 200,000,000 queries. Well, it would if the bomb hadn't just wiped out the entire telephone system as well.

An EMP attack could be launched by terrorists or by someone with a particular grudge against computers. EMPs could also come from space. If so they could hit us at regular intervals. Quite how regular we may be yet to find out. As we have only had electricity for 150 years or so, it is possible we get hit by EMPs from space every 151 years but have never previously noticed.

So if one hits us next year and wipes out the entire electrical system we've built up, we'll be left scratching our heads and saying, "Blimey! That was all a bit of a waste of time then."

TELLTALE SIGNS IT'S HAPPENING
- Your computer will stop working
- Everything else in the world will also stop working

WHERE NOT TO STAND
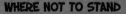
- On the refunds desk at PC World

HOW TO AVOID THE PROBLEM
- Completely encase your computer with lead – and then realize you can't see the screen
- Practise living without computers by moving in with your grandparents

LOOK ON THE BRIGHT SIDE
- You never really got the hang of computers anyway

"This has given me a great idea for a novel."

HOW TO AVOID THE PROBLEM
• Practice playing that *Close Encounters of the Third Kind* tune – they're supposed to like that

LOOK ON THE BRIGHT SIDE
• They're bound to be friendly as long as no-one on our side takes a shot at them first... oh dear

ALIEN INVASION

Invasion of our planet by aliens from outer space would be absolutely horrifying. They would arrive and start blasting us into oblivion one by one or else seize us into slavery while they cruelly take over our world and steal our resources. At least that's what happens whenever we invade anywhere...

It has been pointed out that the universe probably contains at least a billion billion planets. Even if the chance of life emerging on one of these is as little as one in a billion, this means there must be a billion inhabited planets out there.

And yet no-one from any of these planets has so far bothered contacting us even to complain about the noise we're making. We should definitely feel insulted.

Alternatively perhaps the aliens have already visited us incognito, had a look at the mess we've made of things and decided to leave us well alone.

The worry is that space is a bit too quiet. This can only mean one thing. Legions of slobbering green alien invaders are massing somewhere ready to descend on us at any moment and do their worst. On the other hand if these aliens are sufficiently advanced to have travelled across space to reach us they're worth getting to know.

Moving at the fastest speed a human astronaut has ever gone, it would take 26,000 years to travel one light year. The nearest star to us after the sun is 4.3 light years away. So if aliens do turn up they will either be at least 100,000 years old or a ride in their spaceship will be quite exciting.

This also means that any aliens are unlikely to arrive to steal our incredible technological secrets such as the iPod or the hover mower.

On the other hand if they do turn out to be marauding monsters, we can still die safe in the knowledge we are being wiped out by a much more advanced civilization than our own.

TELLTALE SIGNS IT'S HAPPENING
- Flying saucers will be coming out of the sky
- Large numbers of people will be pointing at the sky in the general direction of the flying saucers
- Invasion of little green men who are not involved in any form of performance art

WHERE NOT TO STAND
- Immediately below the flying saucers
- At the head of any impromptu "Welcome To Planet Earth" delegation waiting immediately in front of the flying saucer's doors

ARMAGEDDON

Yes, it's the classic end of the world scenario! According to the end of the world lover's favourite bit of bedtime reading, the *Book of Revelation*, Armageddon will be the site of the final battle between good and evil. If you haven't read the *Book of Revelation* then look away now because we're going to give away the ending

The *Book of Revelation* is a bit like the trailer at the end of the Bible telling us what's coming up next. What Revelation seems to say will happen is a massive, final, mother-of-all-battles between God and Satan at a place called Armageddon. Satan, it is predicted, will have made himself known in the world in the guise of the beast, the anti-Christ or possibly Simon Cowell. After the battle Jesus will return to Earth and rule over us all for 1,000 years until the Last Judgement when God will separate the sheep from the goats and the goats will be severely punished for all their wicked goat-like tendencies. After this there will be much weeping and gnashing of teeth and maybe some bleating.

Unfortunately the *Book of Revelation* is not written in a particularly clear and helpful way and has noticeably failed to win any awards from the Campaign for Plain English or indeed the Campaign for Plain Apocalyptic Prophecies In Ancient Greek. Instead it consists of a series of extraordinary visions, the exact meaning of which no two people have ever agreed on.

Armageddon is however a real place. It's a dusty hill in Israel more commonly known as Tel Megiddo. It was the site of several battles in the years before Christ. More recently at the end of the First World War Allied troops chose it as a site for a battle with the Ottoman Army. Surely when selecting a site for a battle, plumping for Armageddon must have given the participants just a little bit of cause for concern. Presumably, when the proper, final Battle of Armageddon breaks out, God will be destined to win because of the slight advantage He enjoys by virtue of the fact that He is God. If the supreme being of the entire universe shows up one day ready for a bit of a tussle surely it would be a foolish move to join the opposing team no matter what they're offering to pay.

So why don't we all decide now to be on the good side and then hopefully Armageddon will turn out to be a very short, one-sided battle. Although if the battle turns out to be against a solitary Simon Cowell, we could probably keep it going a little bit longer.

TELLTALE SIGNS IT'S HAPPENING
- It will be the end of the world
- The final battle between good and evil should be widely reported

WHERE NOT TO STAND
- On the evil side when the teams are being picked

"This isn't Armageddon... it's a bar brawl on a Saturday night. Let Pestilence read the map."

HOW TO AVOID THE PROBLEM
• Take a note from your mum saying you have a cold and need to be excused from the ultimate battle between good and evil

LOOK ON THE BRIGHT SIDE
• That'll be the ultimate battle between good and evil sorted once and for all

"I'm wasting my time here."

HOW TO AVOID THE PROBLEM
• Request you be transferred into Grand Theft Auto

LOOK ON THE BRIGHT SIDE
• This explains a lot about how weird your life has been
• You could get to meet Sonic the Hedgehog

DISCOVERY THAT WE'RE ALL IN AN ARTIFICIAL REALITY

Statistically it is highly likely that our entire world and everything and everyone in it is not real at all but all part of an artificially created reality. You should never therefore put money on whether you really exist or not.

The argument goes like this. At the moment you can tell if you're looking at a computer generated artificial reality for three reasons. It doesn't look that realistic, you can crash your car as often as you like but still keep driving and, the final giveaway, you have to sit in front of a large humming computer while you watch it.

Computers are however increasing in capability at an apparently unstoppable rate. Eventually therefore computer generated artificial realities will become incredibly realistic. Artificial reality will then be more realistic than reality itself although a glance round at the rest of your family might make you wonder if this hasn't happened already. Eventually there will be multiple artificial reality simulations of everything that has ever happened in history anywhere. This includes you and whatever dubious practices you have got up to during your life.

This means that statistically the world we inhabit is far more likely to be an artificial reality than a genuine one. This is a very annoying form for the end of the world to take because it means that our world has never really existed. Nevertheless we have kept paying our taxes and have never found the button that would have enabled us to do somersaults 20 feet in the air or fire laser beams from our eyeballs.

If we are all in an artificial reality this means that our entire world could be wiped out at any moment by a computer virus or by someone accidentally pressing the off switch.

It also means that there really is a God sitting out there somewhere watching us but unfortunately he is probably a fat spotty computer programmer.

TELLTALE SIGNS IT'S HAPPENING
- You unexpectedly find yourself switched off
- You get the sneaking suspicion someone out there keeps putting you in really weird situations

WHERE NOT TO STAND
- You're not really able to stand anywhere because you don't really exist

97

MATTER SUDDENLY TRANSFORMS INTO SOMETHING ELSE

It would be very disconcerting if matter in the world around us suddenly transformed into something different without any warning. Which of us wouldn't be upset if a friend or loved one suddenly metamorphosed into a giant lobster called Kevin? But then, as we all know, people do change.

At our everyday level of existence matter seems quite stable and tends to behave itself unless it is in the form of teenagers. At the atomic or quantum level however, matter behaves in much more unpredictable and peculiar ways and as a result rarely gets invited out to dinner parties.

We are all aware of Heisenberg's uncertainty principle. This either says, "Blimey! I don't know which one to choose. They all look nice!" or, alternatively, if you look at an atomic particle to see what it's doing and where it's going, the particle will be directly affected by the very act of looking. This principle too applies equally well to teenagers.

The uncertainty that exists at the quantum level leads to the idea that multiple universes may exist. In these multiple universes every possible variation of what could happen at any time gets played out which may account for why we feel so tired all the time.

The behaviour of the matter at the quantum level may mean that universes almost identical to our own exist but in which utterly bizarre things happen. The sun could leap from one side of the sky to the other. People could transform into coffee machines. Countries could unexpectedly turn into custard. Obviously insane things like this don't ever happen in our universe.

There is a theory that if you give an infinite number of monkeys an infinite number of typewriters they will eventually produce the entire works of Shakespeare although they will probably produce the entire works of Jeffrey Archer first. This does however mean that the infinite monkeys will occasionally type the entire works of Shakespeare only for it to suddenly end "To be or not to be... ghkawruebglaneuylhbrrrrkkkyyyyqqqhwsb!"

And there's the problem for us! If the multiple universe theory is correct it means we could all be living in a universe that could at any moment, without any warning whatsoever, suddenly go "ghkawruebglaneuylhbrrrrkkkyyyyqqqhwsb!"

TELLTALE SIGNS IT'S HAPPENING
• Animate and inanimate things around you will start acting even sillier than usual

WHERE NOT TO STAND
• Next to anything likely to transform into something particularly large, particularly smelly or particularly lascivious

"You've changed since we got married."

HOW TO AVOID THE PROBLEM
• Move to a different multiple universe – there should be lots to choose from

LOOK ON THE BRIGHT SIDE
• It explains a lot about how weird the world is

"It's Ragnarok...not anorak!"

RAGNAROK

HOW TO AVOID THE PROBLEM
• Tell them to go home because they're all mythological

LOOK ON THE BRIGHT SIDE
• You could ask Líf and Lífthrasir if they need any help

100

RAGNAROK

Ragnarok is the Armageddon of Norse mythology. So presumably this particular end of the world scenario will look a bit like the time when that Finnish heavy metal band won the Eurovision Song Contest with "Hard Rock Hallelujah".

A thousand years or more ago the Vikings told of Ragnarok. None of us particularly listened at the time because we were in the process of suffering rape and pillage at the hands of some big bearded men in tin hats. Ragnarok is the Viking legend of how the Norse gods will meet their final destiny in a great battle. The Norse gods are those we remember from tales we heard in our childhood such as Thor, Odin and Loki but not Captain Marvel. According to the tale the Earth will come to an end following a series of winters without summer during which the sun will become useless and the world will be flooded with water. This scenario will presumably be accompanied by Scandinavian environmentalists continually popping up to tell us, "Ha! We told you so! In fact we told you so twice!!!"

Yes, with all we know about impending environmental disaster the legend of Ragnarok is now looking strangely likely. Any Vikings still around must be kicking themselves that they didn't take out a long term accumulator bet on the story eventually coming good.

On the other hand maybe it's not such a brilliant prediction. It's a story about disaster from the sun, disaster from the sea, disaster on the land and disaster in a huge final battle. There wasn't room for much more disaster in the Viking world. The only thing they missed out from the story was disaster from accidentally sitting on a tin hat with horns on.

According to the story the world will be flooded before two gorgeous blonde survivors, Lif and Lifthrasir, emerge to re-populate the world anew.

So essentially Ragnarok is the entire history of Scandinavian culture: a big Viking battle followed by environmental disaster and finally something resembling a 1970s porn film.

TELLTALE SIGNS IT'S HAPPENING

• There will be a huge battle between armies of large bearded men but there won't be a motorbike in sight

WHERE NOT TO STAND

• Scandinavia
• On the land, near the sea or anywhere under the sun
• Near anyone wearing a tin hat with horns

SCIENTIFIC EXPERIMENTS GOING WRONG

We naturally assume that all scientists are completely mad. After all, how else can you account for the mad facial hair, floral shirts and over excitement at the slightest glimpse of an equation that they repeatedly exhibited on the Open University?

Dr Jekyll. Dr Frankenstein. Dr Doom. Dr Evil. It could be the list of nominations for next year's Nobel Prize couldn't it? Yes, these are the most famous scientists the world has ever known and yet each of them is insane and obsessed with the destruction of humanity.

We are entranced by and yet fearful of scientists. They are clearly so brilliant that the constant waves of brain energy radiating from their scalps makes their hair stick out in unusual ways. We also know they are absent-minded. They are therefore constantly forgetting simple things like personal hygiene and being careful to avoid any activities that might accidentally destroy the entire world.

It is well known that scientists keep inventing things that could, in the wrong hands, lead to catastrophe such as the atomic bomb, biological weapons and Botox. We are however prepared to tolerate scientists' life-threatening activities at least until they invent a time machine.

Scientists developed the Large Hadron Collider at Cern. This was a fascinating experiment designed to answer some of the greatest questions of science. The entire focus of press attention however was in whether the experiment would accidentally create a black hole which would eat our universe and if so would it be possible to claim compensation afterwards.

After a week and a half of operation, we were all noticeably still here so the Large Hadron Collider had to be switched off and fixed. Scientists! You can't even trust them to destroy the universe properly!

TELLTALE SIGNS IT'S HAPPENING
- Some scientists will look slightly embarrassed
- Some other scientists will look incredibly pleased with themselves
- At least one scientist will be laughing in a traditional evil mad scientist manner

WHERE NOT TO STAND
- Immediately next to any artificially created black holes

102

HOW TO AVOID THE PROBLEM
• Exile all the scientists so we can go back to living according to good, old fashioned, ever reliable superstition
• Get a scientist to give you a highly detailed explanation of what's gone wrong – this will at least have the effect of making your last few moments on Earth feel like they're going on forever

LOOK ON THE BRIGHT SIDE
• There will be a very good scientific explanation for why the universe has just been destroyed
• You might live long enough to see someone given the Nobel Prize for destroying the universe

"I was hoping for more of a desk calender."

HOW TO AVOID THE PROBLEM
• Buy these Mayans a nice new calendar – perhaps one illustrated with puppies

LOOK ON THE BRIGHT SIDE
• If they're right we don't need to buy any Christmas presents in 2012

MAYAN CALENDAR

According to some commentators the world is due to end on December 21, 2012. The reason: this is the final day in the calendar of the ancient Mayan people. For God's sake someone buy these people a new calendar!

The ancient Central American Mayan people came up with a calendar that goes up to a certain point and then stops. Some have concluded that this must mean that the world must be coming to an end on that date. The date in question is December 21, 2012.

Of course everyone else apart from the Mayans have come up with systems of counting and dating that manage to carry on after December 22, 2012. Some even go beyond that. So maybe the fact that the Mayans' calendar runs out doesn't mean that the world will end but rather that the Mayans should get out a bit more and catch up on some of these new fangled systems of counting.

Nevertheless certain New Age types are adamant that the end of the Mayan calendar must mean the end for all of us. But are these Mayans really so clever? What else have the Mayans ever done for us? It wasn't the Mayans who gave us the printing press, electricity or the K-Tel Veg-O-Matic vegetable slicer. So unless they turn out to be the people who thought up mayonnaise, Mayan culture has not proved particularly influential.

December 21, 2012 will admittedly be the winter solstice but then the Mayans were quite good at calculating the duration of the year. They also successfully predicted the year their civilization would be overrun by foreigners. Presumably this was inevitable because these foreigners came armed with slightly more advanced methods of counting.

If, when other calendars are published for 2012, they also stop on December 21, we should start worrying that something's going on. Not only that but why are the only people who know about it all working in the calendar business?

TELLTALE SIGNS IT'S HAPPENING
• One fairly big sign will be that the world will end on December 21, 2012

WHERE NOT TO STAND
• Too near any Mayans when they start celebrating and chanting, "Told you so!"

105

THE RAPTURE

One day you will look around and notice that all your most devout Christian friends suddenly seem to have vanished off the face of the earth. There will only be two possible reasons for this. Either there is a sale on at your local Christian bookshop-cum-tambourine megastore or The Rapture has begun...

The Rapture is an end of the world scenario predicted by certain Christian groups. The reason it is called The Rapture is because they will all be so flipping chuffed when it happens. The Rapture is a twist on the traditional belief in Jesus' second coming. The idea is that Jesus will do his second coming in two goes. The second of these will not however be referred to as a third coming or as second coming 2.1.

The first second coming will be a secret one. This will involve Jesus taking away all genuine believers living and dead. There will then follow a seven-year period of terrible, horrible and deeply unpleasant tribulation for the rest of us while all the true believers watch from the comfort of the heavenly directors' box. Jesus will then do his second coming for a second time. This time the second coming will not be secret and all of us who have suffered the seven years' tribulation will be kicking ourselves.

According to some authorities, the idea of The Rapture only dates back to the 1830s. It was a prediction by a member of a religious sect which found its way into a bible that was widely used in the USA. Rapture devotees disagree with this however and look forward to seeing anyone who puts this evil rumour about suffering in the tribulation.

Various dates have been suggested for The Rapture. Edgar C. Whisenant, a NASA engineer and bible scholar, published a book that gave no less than *88 Reasons Why The Rapture Could Be in 1988*. Don't panic. You didn't miss anything. Whisenant nevertheless managed to sell 4.5 million copies and churned out a series of presumably less successful follow-ups. These included *89 Reasons Why The Rapture Is In 1989* (published 1989), *23 Reasons Why A Pre-Tribulation Rapture Looks Like It Will Occur On Rosh-Hashanah 1993 (1993)* and the more bullishly titled *And Now The Earth's Destruction By Fire, Nuclear Bomb Fire*.

Who knows if The Rapture really will cometh to pass but the worrying thing is there already don't seem to be so many Christians around as there used to be.

TELLTALE SIGNS IT'S HAPPENING
- Christians will disappear from the Earth
- Christians will all be up in the sky looking down and pointing at the rest of us
- Christians up in the sky will have very smug looks on their faces

WHERE NOT TO STAND
- Too close to your DVD of *Life of Brian* In the midst of any group of devil worshippers, heavy metal fans etc

"Then again it could just be a break in the clouds!"

HOW TO AVOID THE PROBLEM
• Try hanging on to Cliff Richard's ankles when he gets hoisted up into the clouds

LOOK ON THE BRIGHT SIDE
• You shouldn't get so many people knocking on your door to talk to you about religion
• It will settle beyond all reasonable doubt who was right and who was wrong God-wise

107

TAKE A DEEP BREATH...

"You promised you wouldn't blow your top."

WE'RE NOT DOOMED... ARE WE?

It's always possible to look on the gloomy side of things but we can't really be doomed can we? It shouldn't be too much of a problem for us to come up with solutions to the problems we face. After all, it was us who created most of them...

We are faced with so many possible ends of the world, it's going to be difficult to fit them all in. We are however an intelligent species. Just how intelligent is clearly demonstrated by the number of brilliant ways we've come up with to destroy our planet. Interesting definition of intelligence that, isn't it?

But never mind! Clearly we are intelligent even though we use this intelligence in incredibly stupid ways. Not only that but we are also survivors. Us and cockroaches.

No matter what has been thrown at us in the past from super-volcanoes to meteorite strikes, bubonic plague to nuclear confrontation, we have always survived. And that's not a claim we would be making if we hadn't... for one very obvious reason.

It's true that we've made a terrible mess of the entire world, threatening both our own survival and that of every other species on Earth. But look on the bright side. We weren't actively trying to bring this environmental catastrophe about. In fact most of the time we were trying to improve things. So just think what state the world would be in if we really *had* been attempting to wreck the place.

In the future we will surely do better. Mankind will come together and work as one to overcome all the terrible problems currently facing us. And once we've done that we can then go back to waging constant, terrible, bloody wars against one another.

So once that's all done, the threat of doom will no longer hang over us. Except of course it will because we know that ultimately all matter in the universe will be torn apart and there's not going to be much getting round that one.

At least it has now been possible to narrow down the exact moment when our doom will occur. Apparently it will happen some time between right this moment and in twenty billion years' time.

Not only that but it's not even clear whether it will be in the morning or the afternoon.

TELLTALE SIGNS WE HAVEN'T BEEN DOOMED SO FAR
- We'll all still be here

WHERE NOT TO STAND
- If anyone ever asks at any stage, "Who'd like to be doomed and who wouldn't", try not to get confused and end up standing on the "doomed" side

"I see a bright, peaceful and serene future."

HOW TO AVOID THE PROBLEM
• You can succumb to doom if you really want

LOOK ON THE BRIGHT SIDE
• If we manage to survive we'll be able to dream up lots of exciting new ways in which to destroy the planet!

THINGS TO SAY IF IT REALLY IS THE END OF THE WORLD

- Oh bollocks!
- Bye everyone!
- Oh no! Just think what this is going do to house prices!
- Cheer up! It's not the end of the world... Oh no. Hang on. It is!
- OK, everyone, even though it's the end of the world let's all try and keep calm and stay positive here!
- I've got a note from my mum so does that mean I can be excused?
- Well, we wasted our money booking next year's holiday early didn't we?
- Do you know what, this kind of thing always happen to me!
- Over there! Coming out of the sky! It's Jesus!... Ha! Made you look!
- I told them this would happen!
- So do you reckon we've just got time for a quickie or what?

THINGS TO SAY IF YOU DISCOVER YOU HAVE JUST UNEXPECTEDLY SURVIVED THE END OF THE WORLD

- Wow! That was cool!
- Well, that could have been a lot worse couldn't it?
- Where have all the people gone?
- Did I just miss something or what?
- OK, everyone, follow me and I will be your leader!
- Let's try and not dwell on the fact that 99.9% of the world's population have all just died! They were clearly all losers and we're better off without them!
- If it's still standing, I bagsy Buckingham Palace!
- Behold! I am the one who commanded the end of the world to stop! Now you must bow down and worship me as your new god!
- Now who do you think we write the letter of complaint to about all this?
- I have just discovered in the rubble a book called *We're All Doomed*! It will be our new Bible!
- OK then, who wants to start re-populating the planet?
- Well if this isn't an excuse for a party I don't know what is!